# ALIENS, GODS & ARTISTS

# ALIENS, GODS & ARTISTS

## SIX STORIES

# SAM EISENSTEIN

First published in 2018
by Eyewear Publishing Ltd
Suite 333, 19-21 Crawford Street
Marylebone, London W1H 1PJ
United Kingdom

*Cover design and typeset by* Edwin Smet
*Author photograph by* Chana Eisenstein, DVM
*Cover painting by* Dan Shupe
*Printed in England by* TJ International Ltd, Padstow, Cornwall

Thank you to Dan Shupe and his agent and gallery for their kind permission to use his painting. We thank Susan Anderson at LA Artists especially. Laartists.com



ISBN 978-1-911335-68-9

*The editor has generally followed American spelling and punctuation at the author's request.*

WWW.EYEWEARPUBLISHING.COM

**To my wife, Bettyrae,**
**for putting up with my fantasies.**

**Warm thanks to all the members**
**of the Gene Stone Writers Group**
**for their patience and good temper.**

Sam Eisenstein
was born in Bakersfield, California, in 1932.
He studied Jungian psychology in Zurich and worked for many years as a teacher and consulting therapist. He has taught at colleges in Los Angeles for over fifty years, is the author of many novels and collections of short stories, as well as a poetry collection, and lives with his wife in Pasadena.

# CONTENTS

# ROLLING THUNDER

I knew something was haywire when my dog cleared his throat, looked directly at me, and said: "This is going to seem a bit peculiar to you, George. I *can* call you George?" He stopped abruptly, with an expression of discomfort.

In a lifetime of loving dogs, putting on them the most complicated of feelings, understandings, all the most caring emotions – well, I like dogs far more than I like most humans, but I've never imagined a dog of mine rising to speech. Still, I wasn't fainting.

"This is very much out of order, you understand. We never interfere directly in human events. That is strictly out of bounds. Like tennis, or prize fighting." it went on, as though I were a complete ninny. "Or hardly ever."

"I know what you're talking about," I replied, with some irritation. "I live here. You're an alien, aren't you? Speaking through my dog?"

A gasp. "I thought I'd have to go through numerous gyrations to get you to understand. I'm glad my agents picked you. Grateful."

As though my dog had become a kind of marionette, he lurched over to me and licked my hand.

"Ugh," he said. "I need to train him not to do that. Very unpleasant."

"My hand is clean," I said. "Can you get to the point? I'm grateful and all that, but certainly you have some cosmic purpose in breaking through the screen that divides us. I already knew there was a greater purpose for our lives here on this pathetic planet. You've proven this for me. It's a shame nobody would believe this. They'd think I'm psychotic. Maybe I am. Maybe you're not really here. Actually, I'd like some proof. Can you give me some?"

"Sure," he or it said, with more assurance, "in time. But for now I need you to be president."

I laughed, bitterly. "We just elected a pompous ass as president. What can you do about that?"

"We need to reset evolution. For millions of your years it has gone forward quite smoothly. But now, with the new one, everything is cockeyed, I'm not prepared to explain it to you."

"I wouldn't understand."

"No insult, but no, you wouldn't. We are millions of times smarter than your species. But that's not the issue. We needed someone ready to put himself out of the running."

"I see you are adept at euphemism. Yes, I was getting ready to kill myself. Are you going to drug me into changing my mind?"

"We know how to simulate sympathy. I will do that in a moment. For now, I want to explain. You have nothing to lose. You've already lost it all. Your precious dog, even, though this one is apparently a fair substitute, as you pet and feed it and take it for walks. Anyway, not important. Your last marriage ended in your wife's accidental death. Your first wife died after a horrible set of illnesses, leaving you an emotional wreck, and her children don't speak to you. Not your fault, apparently. I'm sorry to reuse that word. I know you, as a wordsmith, cherish synonyms. I'll keep that in the forefront."

I was beginning to feel again the short string I was living on, wanting to snap it, even though this thing was kind of interesting, even though it surely wasn't happening.

"Oh, it's happening all right. The purity is what we want. No hope. Especially as your country is on a steep slide to anarchy, revolution or dictatorship. We don't want any of those things to happen. But you have to be prepared to become a neglected hero, divine person, and then martyr. That is death, of course, but you are on track for that anyway, aren't you?"

It actually wagged its tail when saying that last. The eyes of the dog, though, were very sad, as though on a very short chain when the world outside beckoned. Abruptly, I was angry.

"Why don't you take yourself out of the dog and speak to me directly. I can handle it."

The dog looked somber. "I'm not sure you can. One of us has appeared to your type at various times in your history, and this apparition, so-called, led directly to psychosis."

I sniffed. "I'm much better prepared. Try me."

I felt myself lifted, suddenly, beyond anything solid. I was floating. Or else everything was floating. A vague form was in front of, and also surrounding me, neither one distinctly. I tried to think myself on solid ground. But no way. Still, I understood things that before were clear only when I was high on psychedelics. Is that the royal road to the immortals?

"No, it's not. And I need to explain. We have your sort mapped out for years untold for you. We go there at will. Also to the past. But there may be an even more superior race than us that is deliberately sabotaging our plans. What you might call 'turtles all the way down.' And down. And down. Is there an ultimate deity-sort? No way of knowing, unless we stop whatever they are planning on this tiny piece of real estate you call your planet."

"Why do you care?"

"Nobody of our sort knows the answers to that question. Some things are out of our bounds. So, I was sorted out and sent to give you the power to stop the fool from taking office and trashing years of preparation."

"For what?"

"For a formal visit from our hierarchy, something that will deviate your destiny to such an extent that the denizens working to sabotage our plans will be taken unawares and be unable to do what they want to do, whatever that is."

"For all your wisdom, you don't know?"

"I should go back. Yes, we know their plans. But we can't stop them. They are beyond us." The dog scratched his belly, looked speculatively at his organ, sighed and lay down on his front paws. "But we need someone pure. Absolutely without hope. You, in short."

"But now I'm not that anymore. You've given me hope, or at least an interest in going on."

"Paradox, perhaps, but are you willing to give it a go?"

"I see you asking, but I imagine you have the ability to make me think I want to do something even if it's remote."

The denizen said nothing. I know I was being asked, tasked, with looking at my surroundings. Dirty dishes scattered among the plastic and greasy take-outs. Telltale evidence of cockroaches feasting on what I left. Dirty clothes. Of course, it was a slum. I had abandoned a nice house in the suburbs to the ungrateful kids of my first marriage, who were in the process of selling it; I wasn't involved. My job, my pathetic teaching job, was over. Several unsatisfactory notices. With sympathy, but nevertheless, over. Women bearing steamy dishes were finished too. No hope. And the country in a tailspin of greed and stupidity. I needed to get out.

"So, as a psychotic, what do you want me to do? Go around dressed in a bed sheet?"

"As unlikely a place as you could imagine. Kern County. Bakersfield. You know the place?'

"Sure, used to go through it on the way north. Dismal. Dusty. Dead."

"Right. Dead. Like you. Good place to start a resurrection. An insurrection. You will have fierce followers, who will do as you tell them. You will tell them Bakersfield wants to secede from the union."

I snorted. "Sure. Anybody dumb enough to follow that?"

"We don't need intelligence. We need numbers. As with evolution. Requires volume."

"Like buying something in bulk. You're buying us in bulk."

"Precisely," the form said, shifting shape a bit, and, as it did, surrounding me with a very pleasant glow, like after two shots of expensive liquor. Which was then followed by perceptible change, a shift, anxiety entering. It seemed to be going away from me. I was left hanging. It felt precipitate. I felt the thing was abandoning me and I was about to fall. I didn't want to fall. I wanted to kill myself in my own way, not just falling out of a ten-story building height.

"Hey!" I yelled.

It was back. "We have less of your time than I thought," it said, with its tongue out. "Testing the air. Like your snake."

"I don't have a snake," I said with familiar irritation. I was growing comfortable with the presence.

"We are in Bakersfield," it announced. "In Cottonwood Road. You are sixteen."

"Wait! Why am I taken back to my adolescence?"

"Emotions recollected in less than tranquility. You have to be armored."

No idea what that meant. But I saw myself parking my father's 1941 International pickup truck in the mud in front of the shack I had been told contained women who rented out their bodies to all comers. Double meaning intended. I knocked on the wall, as there was only a flap where the door should be. A very little child, mostly naked and dirty, held the flap open without speaking a word. Inside it was dark and smelled of unwashed bodies. A very old woman lay on a kind of plinth. She looked at me without expression. A youngish woman appeared out of the gloom. "Five dollars," she said flatly. "In advance." I was ready and handed it to her. I couldn't speak. I didn't have words. She was as black as the atmosphere. She pulled me over to a bed that sank under her weight. Her head was at the level of my waist. Showing some impatience, she pulled open my belt and yanked my pants down.

"Do I have to remember this in detail?" I spoke to emptiness, choked up.

Then I was somewhere I'd never been in my own life, in front of a large group of people inside a tent, finishing a sermon or lecture or something. People stood up, shouting, whether angry or agreeing I couldn't tell.

I was arguing my case in a room filled with well-dressed people. They murmured. Each had an envelope that everyone opened and marked, then sealed the envelope. Young people went among them and collected the envelopes. They brought them to me. I opened and announced names.

Apparently, there was shock. Murmurs.

Sounds of gunshots outside. Roars. Upset. My dog was barking wildly next to me.

"This is what was necessary to bring your planet back to something approaching equilibrium," it said, apparently only to me.

And then, in another shift of time and personality, I was a woman. A strange feeling between my legs. A vacancy where before I hadn't been aware of a presence. It would take some getting used to. Could I love a man?

"Not relevant, George."

I was seasick, and amid the rolling, I slid, jolted to the side of the ship to throw up. Curious birds and beasts regarded me from their various places where they stood or lay without hindrance but without apparently any desire to move about. My eyes were dim with salt and spray. There was no horizon, no land, no apparent end to the ship, front or back.

"That will be enough experience of the Flood, George. We've got to move at what for will be for you a very fast speed."

Looking at my knuckles was a shock. Blistered, marked with cuts, but still strong, almost obscured by coarse hairs, I was swinging between trees, a roaring from beneath me keeping me aloft and moving. And moving toward another such as me, her arms swinging, vocalizing to try to scare off the predators below. But most important, I had to continue to live, to protect her and the infants. I had such a surge of animal spirits! Suicide! Stupid, selfish idea!

"Yes," I thought I heard a murmuring. "That worked."

Then she was a village girl, dirndl in hand, asking for tutoring in simple German, in which I was more than adept. I caressed her, an old man! But then, I saw my hand again, smooth, unwrinkled, but trembling with desire to touch her unfettered breast. Then we were nearly naked, in a cove or meadow. She was mine. Then weeping, her distended belly pointed at me accusingly. I was speechless. No nouns, no verbs, ridiculous.

"Wait, don't let her die for me. I know this story. It's only a story, isn't it?"

"All your stories take place in one or another of the universes we set up for you. Just let it play," said the voice of my dog, poor innocent as much as the girl!

"What is the purpose of all this?"

"No way for you to understand. And it will all be wiped when I am done," my little dog announced. "Like a dream. A little bit remembered, mostly not. You are doing well."

I was comforted, but uneasy because I was comforted. Used. Manipulated. I stared at the patch of skin on my little dog and was reminded, once more, of the horrible moments my second wife and child suffered, before they died. It was on a happy road trip to Las Vegas to see the Cirque. I had to stay behind, then fly up to join them. They never arrived. It was a big truck, fog, they never had a chance. Fire enveloped the car. They were ejected, burning. Only the dog survived, miraculously, but he will always, until death, bear the scars, partially denuded. Somehow, I hold it against him that he survived. Silly, isn't it? But I can hear their screams before they died. I always hear their screams. Now it remains as a tinnitus, a neurological thing.

"Yes, but if you killed yourself, their memory would die with you," said the resented dog.

"Syllogism. Specious logic. Other people held them dear," I answered, resenting.

"How about life after death?"

"Forget it. You have to know most of us have laughed that off."

Immediately, if not before, there was a lurch and somehow I was in their presence, both of them. They were luminous, illuminated, glowing, surrounding me with their love and affectionate closeness. I was speechless with a kind of combination of exhilaration and dread. I was afraid of them, afraid to touch them, for fear they would fragment.

"Go ahead. Speak to them. They have anticipated this. Not desiring your early death, but ready for it, and your precious dog."

I spoke to them, we were reunited, somehow, our daughter was the age she was when she was killed. Years went by. Where we lived, what we did – all that was a kind of smear.

Then I was back in my pathetic apartment. But not despondent. I had apparently been asleep for a long time, as the dog nudged me, needing to go out. Or be fed. Or cuddled. Responded to. But not occupied. His eyes were clear, and clearly his own. The pills were in their bottle. I didn't feel any need to use them. Something had happened. But it didn't have to be an extraterrestrial. The political situation was just as sour. I had not prevented the ascension of a potential dictator.

Something had happened. I was changed. Could a dream do this? Is there a super-powerful force, immensely more intelligent and able than we are? Able to form our lives to fit their programs for us? Not supernatural, but super-able to travel through dimensions, time, space and personalities?

I will never know, but I anticipate a joyous reunion with my loved ones. That much, totally irrationally, I expect of the future.

# SIBYL

I fled Him, down the nights and down the days;/I fled Him, down the arches of the years;/I fled Him, down the labyrinthine ways/Of my own mind; and in the mist of/ tears/I hid from Him, and under running laughter.... – Francis Thompson, "The Hound of Heaven," 1890

...Away! take heed;/I will abroad./Call in thy death's-head there, tie up thy/fears; He that forbears/To suit and serve his need/Deserves his load./But as I rav'd and grew more fierce and wilde/At every word,/Methought I heard one calling, 'Childe'; /And I reply'd, 'My Lord.' – George Herbert, "The Collar," 1630

Moving is less and less a fuss, the only thing that I can claim has gotten easier as I age.

The day will arrive when even I, cursed with immortality by a god, will be so old my atoms will simply melt, dissolve into my chair, and I will not be noticed at all by the end of a succession of men, one with bulging biceps, who ascend, tramping heavily, to my new garret, garbed in a T-shirt already redolent with sweat, whose wine-dark stains, sourced at the armpit, flows like a fickle river diving into sand above the third rib.

On that day one of the movers, measuring and weighing with his eyes before hoisting my wing-back chair, might perceive me as no more than a sort of bas-relief pattern on the chair bottom, remaining somewhat depressed from the time when I possessed mass, bulk and extension.

If he is feeling raffish, he may decide to carry it upended on his head, appearing to his moderately amused companions like a nun inside an impossibly wide coif. The top of his head will push not painfully into the seat where late my posterior rested. He will not be expecting that this careless action will open a connection between the self-saturated cushion and white tissue convulsing just under his microns-thin skull.

I love watching eyes at the moment when shock widens the pupils, analogous to when nictitating membrane slips over the eyes of other living creatures to cleanse or protect. In that instant, as universal buried knowledge of natural instinct roughly uncovers itself, the stunned moving man sees that what he believed was choice has been part of inelastic broadcloth he cannot take off, remove, or wad into a ball and throw away. The shirt from birth to death is one fabric.

Ever after, the mind of the mover will inhabit a skull that shares space with a shattered and burned-away shutter whose purpose in ordinary folk is to separate images without which life is a continuous blur. With the regularly blinking shutter gone so also disappears the ability to re-establish even rudimentary connection with time. Essentially, I know – and gain sustenance from – what pulses in your bodies and minds.

I await that singularity, one who will find it possible to survive this shock, who calmly removes the chair from his head, sets it down all the while looking directly into my eyes, and extends toward me long shapely fingers with elegant whorls.

No more than a bitter dream. He will not come. It may not matter, as I may not actually sit here waiting but rather sleep somewhere locked in restraints imposed because when awake I attempt to hurt myself.

I am a particle long-ago set in motion by the first fly-swatter, which, entering this universe, randomly knocked a gene askew, and exited leaving behind a trace so slight hundreds of generations passed before an individual with the altered heritage was born disconsolate, orphaned by trillions of parsecs.

I am also that altered individual. But who sees

clearly enough to snip me from the womb? Not my mother, legs spread at my conception, listening to them make the distinctive sweaty tearing sound, skies through blurring tears wheeling with infinite numbers of universes that crack to reveal the face of God my father, in a twinkling lost behind folds of shifting lights.

I don't enjoy seeing his face, yet it is in the mirror. Or do I look into a river, flowing so swiftly as to seem still? Where I stir my finger, a scar appears in the water.

In the opaque water there is nothing to see. Into the same scar you cannot wade twice. Too large for my mother's portal, released by incision, I was born a murderer.

Dreaming I am an egg, I am allowed no time to embrace my shell before the leap into a powers-smaller tadpole scheming to be the one admitted by a universe which opens once then closes forever against every other. I know the bruisers who work security and suffer the acid bath into which gatecrashers are dipped. I make deals on the fly. "Be my springboard, cripple, no good your even entering the race – throw me your germ, I'll make sure it gets in. Your tail, give it to me, mine's crooked or broken, not long enough or too long. Don't ask me what the egg likes. I'll be docile and humble, no hint of my plan once I'm in: to rule."

Thus I brooded (in the cold silent exile of space) strategy, as I foresaw far off turning: my egg.

Whether I see from inside or out, all is in readiness for that one head whose fissures form the mold I was born to fill, soundlessly reaching for his germ containing infinite whirling universes – which I will colonize.

An unpleasant jolt, and I am here. Sitting in the chair. Depressing the chair.

"Where does this one go, ma'am?" the brawny workman asked, mopping his narrow brow with an already-sodden speckled kerchief. The day was steamy for dragging furniture up stairs and through too-small doors.

His head, surrounded by tightly coiled black hair, barely stood out against the water-lined wall. He moved a little to get me better in his sights, peered in at me deep in the dusty obscurity of the room, his unlined face now a spectral white against the dusty velvet drapes a previous tenant had bequeathed me – no boon, as I would presently ask the workman to take them down. Did he have a wife somewhere eager to inherit them?

I trembled. Curious, this emotion. I did not want there to be a wife. And if he had one I mentally wrapped her in suffocating material as a spider's meal.

Already I have regained a little form and shape from sipping like a desert fly from the corners of his eyes and mouth, delicate probes that inform me how recently he has hoisted a draught, whose lips his lips have kissed, and were those lips anxious against his eventual return or languorous after sex, tasting of the instant transfusion of sperm from the whirlpool of her womb to the soft shoals of her mouth? If he loves her, the taste of spunk will not repel, but here and now something indecipherable puckers my lips, strange even for me who has savored a veritable constellation of them, which if thrown to the sky, might, like clams, open and close entire universes, setting wise astronomers to ponder black holes, alternative universes, the end of days, or even regret for having answered correctly my sister Sphinx her riddle, thereby marking thirty to a very useful life.

She was cagey with her killer, desiring to die but careful not to appear to court it, as gods are like children though powerful. Even so, it took years before the slots lined up and she got what she needed – hot-tempered killer, the plague, a city in tatters, the fourth slot wild – but I will bide my time and not present a problem to my bulging carry-on. He appears anyway to be a silent strong type, definitely one to be put off by premature demand. In fact, I observe a bulge in his cheek where a powerful charge of tobacco is stationed, ready to resist invasion by mouth.

"Any particular place you'd like to sit, lady?" he enquired, shrewdly kind, calculating to up the size of his tip, certain of one because of previous solicitude.

I squinted in the intensity of my need to keep him in sight despite the degree of his levels beneath me, while exulting in his rude power, like though infinitely less than the one who planted me.

"Here in the wing-back chair will be fine," I said with a whispery sibilance that I know from experience carries a charge in the absence of a real aroma. Dried to a powder, I couldn't rub two pheromones together. I barked a short laugh audible only to myself. Of course I had tried! Anything. Like a grasshopper I ground my legs to produce a chirping smell to no avail. My curse was profound, wide as well as mocking. You don't turn down a god without certain disadvantages accruing like negative interest.

I had never taken up residence in a used building, nor departed except at the poised threat of a wrecking ball. Neither had my windows' virgin nakedness been obscured by coy coverings. It was an enduring foolishness of mine that some day, as I sat framed, I might catch a glimpse of my godly seducer in the sky or tripping disguised out of a subway station. That he might be arrested by the sight of me? To what purpose? Pity? Desire again? Lust, as I construed it only, never love, not from a god, used to getting his way and then off to newer novelty. Never! Virgin a dozen times over. Virgin temptress forever young to mock his callow frippery, though a god.

So in my arrogance I demanded the boon of immortality, at least as many years as grains of sand in the hourglass. Smiling – how I remember the subtle smile not unmixed with sadness that pulled at my heart so that I misgave the cruel straight line of my lips, my tongue within quivering like the string of a bow ready to shoot mocking contemptuous words – he reminded me of what I hadn't asked to go with the shining sands. What arrogance! To tell me!

But I did not know, and thus sit here immaterial as the dust motes dancing insensate of the stars from which they descend, luckier than me, because they lack memory of their fallen estate. He will never return. They never pass the same place twice. He dipped his finger, made the scar, withdrew to test the wind and set his sail.

Perhaps the sand makes its deliberate way through the pinched waist of the glass only to be turned over to begin again. It happened to another relation of mine, Sisyphus, for much the same reasons.

I like the arrogance of this man in the room with me. "What is your name?"

"Ben," came the reply muffled in the folds of velvet over one shoulder, giving him the momentary appearance of a Roman consul. "Name's Ben. If you need me, I usually hang around the subway entrance or at the coffee shop down the block. That's where you get day labor. If I'm not there, ask someone. For Ben. People generally know where I can be found."

"For Ben," I repeated slowly. "I will remember."

"That's everything," Ben said, "much obliged for the drapes if you're sure you don't want them," and waited, a little nervous, I think, for the answer.

"But don't give them to your wife," I said, repenting casual cruelty, "sell them and get her something nice. Who knows what kind of disease they could carry." I knew. Though my poisonous envy had put it there removal was beyond my scope.

"Not to worry," came the gruff response, "I don't give the ex anything the law don't tell me I have to."

I continued with an orbiting patter of questions around his ears, and like a starving water bug that has impaled and begins to liquefy the insides of a frog before ingesting it though her straw of a tongue, my outline began to firm while Ben lost a trifling mount of bulk.

Exulting in re-acquired scent, I was newly able to embrace his. Invisible tendrils whirled about like a ballroom full of waltzing and merging ghosts.

Bewildered, he shifted his burden grown oddly heavier.

"Don't worry, young man, I have decided to offer you extended employment."

Of course there would be further testing. Mold, egg, scissors, gaping abdomen are never enough in themselves.

"Do the children visit you or the other way around?" I asked, hazarding a guess. Children pry deeply into matters, and at the point when even a lug like Ben must finally pay attention the story may still be too frail to stand scrutiny.

Above all he must never catch a true whiff of me, so age-old as to be beyond decay. When young Tut's tomb was opened, the real curse was breathing in the giddy centuries, opening to a vista of a day in the life of death.

It is not in my plan to suck his life into mine, then leave him, empty skin, to form a pattern in the rug or bas-relief next to me in the wingback chair like a hollowed-out Moore couple.

Once a day when the god tilts his sun just right I am allowed to see the hourglass with her impossibly pinched waist daintily eating and digesting my life. As if for my continuing education she tilts to become a mantis chewing steadily through the pate of her mate, while he ecstatically pumps seed to populate a future landscape.

As if these sights are not enough to remind me of what could have been if I had offered up my stoppered vial for sampling, I am made to cringe in a cramp that looks so much like a bow to my young visitor that he answers with his own, grinning all over his face, peeping up at me from under it like a child playing a game, which it is for him. What does he care? A job lasting not quite a day, and now what? What kind of job? He sees nothing of the jet-black eagle voraciously plucking my liver from its wine-dark blood-filled cavity.

It is a story that repeats, for my edification, every day.

Ben looks diffidently around the room, mostly still bare despite several trips with his hand-truck. Carnal matters are far from his mind. More to his liking would be a frosty one.

"Help yourself to a lager from the fridge," I prompt.

"Sure thing, lady. Thanks. Uhh, what do you have in mind? For the job, I mean. It don't look like you've got much to do." Then he hastened to add, "Not that I couldn't feature a steady job. Winter's coming and it gets kinda cold out there."

He ran his eyes over me carefully, estimating how much time I actually had left. I shivered. Lucky his eyes had not stopped even for a second on that part of me I never allowed to be scrutinized. If he had, this Ben of mine would have been dismissed to outer cold. Winter indeed! He hasn't seen a winter like the one I could provide!

From the kitchen, his clear confident voice: "How long do you have in mind?" Emerging with the bottle, he explained, "It didn't really have time to get cold, but that's all right." He took a long swallow, removed the bottle from his mouth and wiped his lips with his left forearm, leaving a long trail on it not unlike that of a snail.

I shivered. If I was to put a new plan in motion I would have to stop painting the animal world over every movement and habit of this Ben. He was human. I am human. For now.

But that's not true, I cried out in pain inside myself. I was human once. I sat on a tulip-bedecked hillock and watched a rainbow approach as a rainbow never can, because the rain had long since departed, fled, perhaps, from before the hot valor of the god. When he finally came nigh it was not as rainbow, nor stallion with thick white and black-flecked tail I saw from far off, but a kind of combination of the two, and also something of my ancient father, too frail to go abroad more than to worship the morning and dusk. My mother, long-since dead, buried, I brought flowers to her simple grave every day, and later told my father of it. I had no friends, and that's a pity, because they might have warned me, or lied, promising me what I could have if only I consented. Even if not made over into a goddess, and who wanted that? Such as they had to present themselves all the time at court, wear stiff clothes, or spend their time in gossip. When would I be able to tend to the grave, or my father so long as he lived? His breath was infinitely dear to me as much for itself as that it still retained something of my mother's as I tucked him in at night, both of us happy if a little wry about the reversal of roles. When I kissed him there remained a dusky hint of my mother's breath from his mouth. And then the day arrived when his lips had grown so cracked he could barely bring himself to even lightly touch my cheek. I grieved in advance.

He could have offered my father a little something to ease his pain, but all his attention was fixed on me, and on that one part of me, the part my mother used to explain was to be consecrated to a future husband, a shallow boy arriving with a bedraggled bouquet, blushing furiously. I valued such a bargain as little as the privilege of being bedded by an immortal. How ironic that I am now as immortal as any mortal ever was.

Yet, he could have taken me when swooning. They do that. Or mount me as swan or bull or even a glittering cascade of gold. I'm not sure to this day I did the right thing, I'm not even sure he was such a devil, that god, because he did not use force. But neither did he force Cassandra. Were we his little joke? Two of his dirtier little secrets? What he could have done!

My mother's whispering to me from the grave – was she all wrong? – continues even as I watch the shaggy mortal out of the corner of one eye. Is there something I will learn from Ben, a child of sorrow, that I don't already know?

Who was growing impatient at this protracted staring through him. He finished his beer and noisily deposited it in the kitchen waste basket and stood, waiting for the words, though he didn't know it, that might change the directions of both our lives, showing that he didn't particularly care, one direction was as good as another for him.

I wheeled myself to the window that faced the street. Yes, my wicker wingback chair had wheels, an antique kind of ambulation.

"This may seem odd to you, young man, but I will be spending a good part of every day here, watching."

Yes, I must be in plain sight of this fissure in earth or pavement, at least two storeys up, not so far that my no longer acute eyesight cannot discern a particular face emerging from the underground, but not so near as to alert a certain one erupting from the underworld, percolating through the soil, once a place of great familiarity to me though now forbidden.

That's how I found him, my carrier, in the old place, emerging from below, like a birth, between the iron thighs of the subway, and I made haste to snag him before he could get away. It turned out there was no need to hurry, as he stopped at the entrance to light a cigarette and to affix a sign around his neck advertising his availability.

"What will I be doing, ma'am?"

"The sign I saw you put around your neck, it was quite well-printed, attractive. Where did you learn to do that?"

He shrugged, but I could tell he was pleased. "Went to art school for a while. About the only useful thing I learned."

"A centaur repairing a toilet. Quite a concept, I'd say."

"Mostly copied from Picasso, ma'am, nothing to brag about."

I wheeled my chair about to look straight up at him in the gathering obscurity. Clouds had covered the sun, and grumbles of thunder ricocheted through the brick and stone canyons, as though the storm were clearing its throat before voicing its intentions.

People were moving along, eager to get to shelter before the rain. Ben turned away from the window, as if by not looking he could deny the storm.

"Do you have a place to go, Ben?"

He clamped his jaw, ready to reject any need, thought better of it, and lowered his head deferentially. It was painful to see the big man doing that. "With the money you pay me, ma'am, I can get myself a room."

"I have a proposition for you, Ben. This flat has two bedrooms. I could offer you one of them, but you would have to be available to perform a certain function. You may not be willing to do it. Do I have your attention yet?"

"I'm listening. But nothing illegal. I've been in jail and didn't take to it."

"Nothing illegal, no. Could you paint and letter a sign with a figure on it of a seer, a prophetess, a sibyl? Even a fortune-teller would be all right."

"I could do that," he answered cautiously. "Not a big deal. Is that all?"

"No. I would need you to hang it around your neck like the sign I saw you wearing and stand at the entrance to the subway, offering my services."

"So you're a fortune-teller." He appraised me. "You don't look like a gypsy."

"What do I look like, Ben?" My heart felt as though something was squeezing it. Not that I found the brute attractive, I was dizzy because he had looked at me, his eyes had not slid off my face and body as though no purchase were possible on so featureless a surface. His glance had stopped, calculated the shape and form of me, and came to a quotient – admission of shape and form.

He shrugged, afraid he had gone too far, I might be insulted. I pitied him. He was lost too, but he would die, nobody would prevent that, nobody stop him from lying down one night, tired out, every muscle and connection whimpering after a lifetime spent in others' service lifting, hauling, tugging, scraping. All at once, as a result of a vote taken in secrecy, they would all let go at once. Maybe like rubber bands every released tension in his body would put itself in the service of sending his spirit aloft. He might even be allowed to be aware in that moment.

He is infinitely better off than me, I thought, throwing him a smile I hoped was reassuring. "All you have to do is stand around and show people where to come. I can use the money. I'll pay you for your time. You'll shop for me. Keep the place clean. All legal."

He glanced at the drapes.

"You must know a place to sell those rags. I don't want the money. They are all yours. Not now. Don't go now, not in the storm."

I'm not sure but that he would have found my proposition too weird even for him if the storm had not already begun, wind whipping gusts of dirty paper and Styrofoam cups into sodden dancers.

The gutters and downspouts weighed in with their varied voices. I saw Ben's lips moving, but with all the racket I couldn't make out words. He realized that and made a dumb show of drawing. I made gestures of giving him money to buy paper when it was dry outside.

"Do you want tea or coffee?" he yelled.

That had to mean he had decided. He was ready to settle in.

Lightning tore the dark to light up a billboard placed right outside my window on the roof opposite. "If you don't show it, who will know it? Strut your stuff," it read, and to illustrate, the artist provided a barely pubescent elegant child on the arm of a leering old man whose stomach even under compression overflowed a too-tight tuxedo. The babe displayed a smile that managed to be so young it could be both innocent and knowing. The immortal couple was shown stepping into a chauffeur-driven limousine. Stroboscopic lightning bursts lent to the scene an impression of movement.

The maker of the billboard was not interested in pursuing the action once the man and girl got into the car and the doors closed on them, but I knew. That leering man would take possession of his prize, rip off her clothes – he had paid for them, so didn't he have the right?

"You can resist," I cried, forgetting Ben was in the room.

"What's that you say, ma'am?" he shouted, not understanding, but uneasy observing my passionate outburst.

"She doesn't have to go through with it. Look," I wheeled about so violently Ben had to skip awkwardly out of the way to keep from being rolled over. "He doesn't care anything about her except she's virgin and beautiful. Her parents can't protect her. In fact, they probably sold her to him."

Helpless rage racked me. He was responsible for the billboard, an example of taunting by the one who never forgave the insult of my refusal.

Ben looked out the window. He turned slowly, a familiar cautious look to which I had quickly grown accustomed written on his face. It meant he would humor me.

"No people walking around out there, lady, everybody's scattered to their burrow." He swaggered a little over his joke. "Is that what you're talking about?"

I pointed with trembling finger at the billboard. His eye followed. I also looked, ready with a compressed lip of contempt. Too late. The trickster, having had his fun, had removed himself. There was left only the picture of an elegantly uniformed man and woman being looked up to proudly by their little girl, who held a crude model airplane in her chubby little hand. Sleek war planes flashed by, appearing no more deadly than dragonflies. "Be all you can be" was the logo.

"Get your things," I commanded.

"That won't take long," Ben answered quietly. "Is there anything you want?"

"Bring me death," I said, smiling.

"Sure thing. Any particular brand?"

"That kind, on the billboard," I answered, wondering if he had heard right.

Considering his cheeriness and the alacrity with which he made to fulfill my demands, he hadn't. Nobody cares to live with a crazy, not even one who is homeless. Demons in residence in his head are enough – he doesn't need or want someone else's to take up space there too. Also, the wildernesses might fight for primacy, even as I did when I refused the first and only one. Even when a man appeared to be someone else, down long vacant years, I knew it was really him.

How do I know Ben is not another manifestation of my ancient mind? The short answer is, I don't, but I am tired. If Ben is the trickster, it could be he is here because he's decided it's time to call it off, as the bosom of the hourglass empties and droops as mine did, and as she grows ever more transparent, shamefacedly unable to keep herself decently covered, maybe the game stales.

In short order, Ben turned out a workmanlike sign. As sun sliced impatiently through the clouds, Ben was out on the sidewalk at the entrance of the subway. To my surprise and dismay, he was wearing one section of purple drape, like a toga, against his bare skin. It would not kill him, not right away, but like radiation it was already at work on his cells, would ineluctably alter them, turn them into something else, a resident enemy that, awakening, will seize the reins and rule.

Again: rule. He wanted to be ruler of my heart and body. He would take no less. With his history of refusals, and I was by no means the first, you would think he'd learn to be more demanding, brutal, like his fellow gods, but he never was. He pursued and forever she was fair. And he was fair. He wore refusal on his head like a diadem, a laurel wreath.

Ben, below happily importuning damp pedestrians, consented to be ruled by me. I would not be as docile. I would be able to knead him. He would get used to me. My demands would grow imperceptibly. Finally, he would find the act inevitable.

Kill me.

I would have to bring him to it before he himself grew too weak. My stupidity about the drapes only compounded my life-long ability to make wrong decisions while predicting accurately future events for others.

Cassandra. Do I know myself? Am I truly myself? And does it matter what I used to be called, in those days when the sun was altogether more brilliant? Mankind then had no ability to loft into the atmosphere the yellow mucus that runs from the noses of his factories. Horses then and cows made the most methane.

While I was thinking, Ben had brought up his

few possessions, including a shopping cart. The rain had washed it, it sparkled. As a carrier for dirty rain-dark clothing and a few shaving things, it was like shabby worn peasants worshiping in a cathedral glittering with gold.

Already there came a knock on the door – timid, almost inaudible, as though the person knocking hoped for no response.

I had to make my living, now our living, with what happened next. Could this be stage fright I was feeling? No, amazingly, it was more like that terror that came over me as I sat with my sisters at a picnic in a leafy bower the first time he approached. I thought then I was the least of my sisters – nobody would single me out, but he did and led me by an unresisting hand through grove after grove of his tree, which gave off the pungent but fresh smell of green, intensities of green, one on another, like mirrors, an infinity of green, and then I saw he was also wearing the leaves. Laughing, he offered to teach me to weave so that I could wear one too. "No," I said, "I've been too long away from my sisters. People will gossip. I'm only a girl." I trembled with – indignation? No, it was something else, a fear of change, of transformation. I knew the man before me meant change, to something I was not. But also he gave off the bitterness of laurel, which when boiled emanates a slick and gummy essence, said to cure ailments of eyes and the privates.

His tree. Was the essence of that other girl coiled around every twig? Sorrowful? No, at peace. The juice also stilled pain, an intoxicant, like those administered by his brother. I realized they are not set against one another, he and Dionysus. I wished for a sister to help me. I was too weak by myself. I wanted to stay with my family, with sisters. Were there ever brothers? I no longer know, I have forgotten. If so, could they have been like Ben? Is that why I was so immediately taken with him?

I looked through the streaked window. *I will have him wash them.* He would do that. I looked at him importuning passers-by, even those he surely knew would be impervious to his entreaties, having his joke. I would need to instruct him to stop. With one customer already with me in the room another woman might be too shy to wait in the other.

She. I already knew that. Soft knuckles hurting on the wooden door told me. Timid, yearning, afraid.

But also believing in the ridiculous possibility that I am the real thing, a seer – never mind I live upstairs from a delicatessen in a dingy apartment building, could I be the one to wrap up and hand her the truth that explains the inexplicable that has eluded her all her life, all twenty minutes of it? Faith in this day and age! Not really so astonishing with the young accustomed to casual encounters on the web, where you find Perseus next to and uniting with pussy, because nobody can spell anymore. It doesn't care how you ache for real not virtual touch but cannot find it, and that, finally disgusted, your own skin crawls away from you for a little peace. The Internet will tell you everything you never knew you needed to know, like Madame Sosostris, but you must view the winking and blinking billboard imploring you to press down – here and here and here, like someone with an itchy back.

I pressed palms flat on the door on the other side of which stood my slender prisoner-to-be, then yanked them back, burning.

She touched the door as though caressing it from her side, pleading her case with fingers touching the sentinel that guards a very secret and important place, perhaps even the entrance to a temple hallowed by age, as the door's darkened wood attested to its dignified antiquity, not years of holding in or out the odors of cabbage, stringy meat, and garbage.

She explored the door like one unseeing. Was she blind? Had some god touched her eyes to keep her from premature knowledge as I in my time was kept from essential knowledge? My elders knew he was after me, but I was allowed to occupy myself with garlands woven from every flower, thrilled when praised for the mosaic I made of them. Even butterflies and other colorful insects alighted on them and made accidental patterns or details we all clapped our hands about.

Like this girl on the other side of the door, I had no breasts to delay the uncaring swoop of my expansive gestures, and when I rolled on the cool grass it was as a complete round, not a thing with lumps on one side to hinder carefree motion.

Was the room ready enough? A little tripod lay all in a jumble on the floor. Ben had either not known how to put it together or felt it was a thing for me to do myself.

I yanked myself forward and with the momentum stepped out of my chair. Yes, I can walk when I have to, but it takes precious energy. Now I was recklessly expending it because I had Ben in reserve. I bent trembling to put it together. Where was a lump of incense? Something had to burn.

The gentle knocking resumed. I couldn't let her in without smoke to soften water marks on the ceiling, graffiti on the walls, tamp the odor, seduce the senses. Looking about, my eye fell on Ben's possessions, his sack of chewing tobacco right on top. I grabbed the sack and emptied it into the little dish on top of the tripod. I would buy him a new one. Matches? Right in the sack! Very practical, Ben.

"One moment," I called as cheerfully as breathless haste allowed. This was a command performance. Never mind that it was on my command, once history is set in motion inertia takes over and one can but try to stay in front of and try to outrun events.

Vexation! Only one chair in the entire apartment. There had been no time to send Ben to scrounge on garbage day or check the thrift stores. One of us would take the chair, but the other? Only the depleted nest of drapes, those Ben had not removed. It would have to do. If I sent her away there would be no telling when or if she returned. It had to be this one, this day.

A tremor ran through me, as though an internal earthquake tipped me slightly off my previous foundation. Rivers in the interior slopped up hard against one bank, leaving the opposite one littered with gasping sea life exposed high and dry. With accumulated force eons hence many rivers within me would, whispering, abandon their former beds altogether.

I shivered. Was I doomed to remain to observe that event, witness the very moment when the last of my bone-littered river channels finally meandered beyond hope of flowing back over its customary bed, carelessly abandoned to dry and crust, to lust bedazzled after a virgin bottom never before watered.

A virgin path.

I put one hand back on the door, slightly warm from hers. It felt as though our fingers had melted the wood and touched.

She passed the last test and was, improbably, virgin.

Just as I put my hand on the handle to open the door I heard heavy steps, a muffled deep voice saying, "Just turn the handle, honey, it sticks a little; I haven't had a chance to get to it. By the time you leave it'll turn easy."

An eternity from now, or now. The gods casually chop time as fine as they slice *kremmýdia* for salad, or fling it with abandon into the boiling pot for a sacred sacrifice offering to themselves. Can one ring of an onion speak to another? What I remember, my long solitary life, may never have been lived by me, be no more than passing dizziness while he held me prisoner in the field teased with a laurel wreath, which for him, as I brood on it, signaled the crown of defeat as much or more than triumph. Since all he got was a crown of laurel, not the girl.

At this moment, I may still be that child as well as virgin, all this waiting around for his return no more than dream. He can do this. Stories are told.

Not precisely punishment or lacking in enjoyment, these years. While a mysterious metamorphosis transforms an entity so big as to be unnoticed to one vanishingly small an interim offers itself during which a body is visible. As each of the ancient worlds wobbled and fell into the sun I spun out of its orbit just in time, suddenly appearing to universal bewilderment in one scene after another until, when it came on the market, I made myself American.

Shrines hereabout do not smell of ripe bodies. Assiduous vacuuming embargoes the slow-building accretion of ancestor debris, whose lives terminated so abruptly the sound of blood remained in the air as an aerosol. But not here, where detergents more than atheism efface the trail gods are used to leave behind them, in a vain hope for followers.

Could it be woeful, bitter and wasted me, the last living mouthpiece of god? The sole ancient who still knows how to shape an altar from dust?

And for what or whom? If Apollo is gone – never say dead – and I scheme and plan for nothing?

Flinging wide the door, another wall met my

eyes – the girl, whose body extended well beyond the frame. I should have caught the tone, that certain something in Ben's voice – pity, contempt, finally even fear, which the American male harbors for mountainous female flesh.

I knew why she remained virgin; her hymen was locked deep within unapproachable thighs. Did she grow jailors' flesh to safeguard the membrane, or was the thing preserved accidentally by gluttony?

Her standing there reassured me the gods still lived – nothing else was capable of such a cruel joke.

Even so hot a body as Ben wouldn't get close enough to touch her. He merely showed her the way in, through which she sidled sideways, daintily for so large a figure, sucking in her cascading bosom which nonetheless stuck and held against the door jamb until releasing with an audible hiss of organdy, a shiny material combined with crinoline making her a pathetic caricature of Little Bo Peep, for which she lacked only the shepherd's crook.

Was I being shown what I really looked like, what I really was? If my refusal took flesh would it look like this?

She looked at me and around the room with sorrow born of experience – nothing would be sturdy enough for her to sit on. Asking a brief permission with her eyes, she found a corner, minced toward it on impossibly slender graceful ankles, and dropped like a balloon deflating, yet even here from long habit holding her legs tightly together.

"I'll get right to the point, madame," her voice starting out as a booming alcoholic basso that nearly flung my chair with me out the window and then wandered toward the upper registers as though unable to decide whether she was a stevedore or one of Sullivan's little girls from school. "What's your specialty – hypnotism, auto-suggestion, avoidance counseling? I've had them all. No good. I was stranded in a rowboat on the Aegean Sea for two weeks and when they found me I weighed more than when I fell in."

"How did you fall in?" I asked.

Her face was perfect, a sphere. Looking at her, I felt I was viewing an archaic rendering of the sun, only with human features. Was she part of a story involving the spurned god I didn't know? If Daphne running had put on leaves and bark, did this one eat while she fled, to protect her virginity encapsulated it in fat?

Or were they all really me, one bead of water splashed into many?

"It was a wedding voyage," the girl said dreamily, "mine. Not that I wanted or was ready for it. A girl of twelve, what does she know but weaving garlands? But how would you remember something like that at your age?"

"I hope you managed to weave more than you killed," I tartly replied, because she had drawn blood, but with her instant crestfallen look I saw she hadn't meant any harm, I was being cruel and wrong. She was only making conversation, motivated by the desire to sound me out. She needed to know what kind of charlatan it was who could be at home in an upper story fish-and-pastrami-smelling space.

"Until that time I was a reed dancing along with the music of any gust of wind," she continued, "a storm was for me a symphony. I was so swift and nimble people remarked how I had no cares for gravity. A surface was a thing to be pushed off from. Yet beneath my joy ticked a time bomb. I could not always remain twelve. I was a block of unincised marble, a bust set upon a pedestal, unconnected to what was hidden between my legs. Then the great sculptor Time began to chisel on me a shape that could not be hidden."

Flowery talk from a blown flower! Maybe just another girl sniffing out a cheap cure for obesity. I have been wrong before. Every oddity presents itself as a unique opportunity to summon forces that made me immortal without giving me reason to be. Why should the god be inclined to do me a favor?

Yet, this girl fiercely guarded her virginity, like me, not on account of anything religious, not coveting sainthood, martyrdom, something silly.

When there were people still living who knew my story first hand, I was often asked, "What was so special about your virginity?" I blushed, having no answer, and the question made it resemble a product, a basket of dates, a paper of figs, something to be bartered.

And everybody had it, nothing unique, not mysterious. Girls my age married as a matter of course, straight out of the nursery into the husband's bedchamber.

No, what made it special is that the god sought it, and having done so, etched a path in that marble for the river of my life to follow. He caused me to refuse. I wouldn't have had the strength but that he gave it me – to refuse. He wanted it so. He wanted me to refuse him? But how could it be otherwise? If he gave my sister the gift of prophecy, he had to have it himself first, no? And to muddy it he had to be able to know what confusion he caused, because he stands above the dimension we live in, he steps over walls as though there were no roof, time, covering our actions.

So if I desired to preserve the fleshy flower

between my legs, secure since before my birth, sleeping at peace, it meant that I had to become its guardian, a priestess, yet it was always dedicated to him. What this means is that I have spent my lifetime in his service when I thought I had escaped him.

How foolish I have been! This girl, a block of sweating flesh squatting in the corner, has forced me to confront what I have up to now avoided.

What kind of power does she possess, this simple looking thing? I must look at her more carefully. Perhaps she is, finally, the agent for a real turn of events.

"What do you want from me? Did you lose it to the fishes, your hoarded-up treasure?" Of course I knew it was still with her but was curious to hear the story of her escape.

"I can't even really tell, so much time has gone by since I could even get near it. Lately, however, I sense I am diminishing in size, withering away and regaining the shape if not the carelessness of the girl I was. If this goes on I am afraid my husband who has never stopped looking will stumble upon me, recognize the wife who jumped ship, seize me, and this time never let me go."

I could have told her that, once past, the god does not return. I could repeat for her the story of fingers in moving water, but it may not hold in her case. I was a girl in a time when gods walked the earth openly. Almost everybody had a tale of personal encounter with one. Discounting ninety percent still left a few credible eyewitness accounts. It surprised nobody when the god hit on me. But this was a modern female.

A fine symmetry grew like a filigree and shimmered between us.

Her flesh, fragrant or noisome, had it actually been able to attract a god? Or was the bridegroom she fled a mere mortal routinely hungry for the taste of unbitten apple, chewing with juice running thoughtlessly down his chin until he reached the core and tossed it, eager to get away to his drinking companions?

Time would tell. Walls were no hindrance to a god's equipment for ferreting out a potential partner.

"You'll think I'm crazy, but I'm not sure my husband is actually a human being. What could he be, then, a devil? There aren't any devils any more, though maybe there used to be. I've read about devils taking human form. The man who married me bought me fair and square from my parents. Where I come from this is usual and natural. But I was a reader, I knew life could be different in other places. Does this explain anything? I jumped overboard. A sailor who saw me untethered a lifeboat.

I saw him looking at me many times while he was at his work. I felt we knew one another without ever exchanging a word. Your serving man resembles him. He does, really. No, I don't say that to flatter. He really does. I've always wanted to thank that sailor for saving me, and lacking opportunity to do that, I would thank your serving man. Isn't that silly? To gush gratitude over a total stranger for a kindness done by a look-alike thousands of miles and so many years ago?"

A scratching like mice interrupted her flow of thought.

"Ben is repairing the door," I said. "Listening at it too, maybe, he could have heard what you said. On the other hand he may have little need to eavesdrop. Do you want me to ask him if he might be willing to help you to lose what no longer has value for you?"

"Would lying with him truly be enough to make the other one stop haunting me?" she whispered.

What did I really think? Maybe nothing more than a half-crazy, fat, hysterical girl? That the ever-scheming god was disguised as Ben? All that would be too neat, too convenient.

Let's figure that all we have here are two women and a homeless man. What would be lost if I got him to take the girl, one virgin as good as another? It might even make enough of a diversion for him to forgive me.

That would turn me into a pimp, I thought, my face showing disapproval at my own plan; a virgin-pimp, selling her again, betraying her no less than her father had. Defensively, I thought: she doesn't risk immortality, what transpired between her and the god on the ship was inconsequential. This mating, equally minor, would find no place in the stories people told.

"Gods are attracted to and take only virgins," I replied briskly, not remembering exactly which one of the girl's concerns I was responding to. "With them size is no consideration, but they never plow a field or travel a road already walked," I said. "Let's assume your bridegroom wasn't devilish. A devil wouldn't have waited, and a mere mortal would not be so patient either. Perhaps a god has special plans for you." Better lay it on thick. "I am aware," I said drily, "that sheer weight never stopped a god. Think cow, Io, Hathor."

References made no difference to her, she plunged right on with her story. "It was my time of month when I jumped into the water. In a matter of hours the bottom of my frail vessel was entirely covered in blood. I was afraid the brilliant red standing out would make it easy for him to turn the ship about and track me down. I scrubbed with what was left of my clothes until I had nothing left on my body. My worry that I would be rescued by my husband turned to fears of being rescued by others who would see me naked and want to rape me."

"Your sense of your own desirability leaves nothing to be desired," I said, silently admitting to once having harbored similar thoughts.

"I buried what remained of my blood in flesh, madame, but every day the irresistible blood swarms closer to the surface. Soon it will be sufficient to broadcast my scent," she cried. "Even my new name, Danaid, won't be adequate to keep him away."

"Nothing will keep him away if what he desires is here, just as nothing will bring him if he has business elsewhere."

"Door's fixed, ladies," Ben bellowed, not failing while opening it to take in with a quick glance the two of us tensely crouching. As he coolly raked his eyes over us, revealing nothing, I'm not sure which of us flinched more obviously. Golden sweat shone on Ben's upper arms illuminated as though by interior light. With a god this would be literally true, not metaphor. All my life long I have never been sure which I was living. What confusion!

A stroboscopic flash ended the momentary standoff. By reflex, I swiveled around to the window where the billboard was sending out spaced bursts like a runway at night. Spread across its surface, a raft of black crows intermingled with naked winged men raced a train across verdant terrain. It was clear that the earth-bound train was no match for the mixed flock of feathered men and birds, but neither was anyone on it even aware of another world threatening it from above.

"Change that sign real often, do they?"

"Ben, go find me another chair, please," I ordered shakily, really more a pleading. Was he aware of his power to do with us whatever he desired? No way either of us could get around him, run far or even escape from the room.

If the god caused the billboard to shift and change, it was for a particular purpose, not amusement, to cause me renewed pain and anguish. I know the time will never come when he leaves me alone. Long ago, if I had bent to his will, his delirament with me would certainly have given way to other ruling passions, conquests. But as the dead letter of his failure still resided within me, very likely grown radioactive after the fashion of these times, he has caused a wave to wash up on my shore: this recreant, another criminal fugitive from the iron male hand.

Did the god enter into the spirit of a time-bound man so that when, with behind-the-scenes help, he finally tracks his tub of lard to my lair the spurned and humiliated bridegroom will flail about indiscriminately, punishing me as well in his maddened charge? Coming to his senses in a scene of devastation of his making, the man not the god will have to take the rap, whining, "I didn't know what I was doing."

Another way of demonstrating his famous undeserved reputation for not consulting his omniscience?

The legend on the billboard now read: "Yesterday, brute force was enough to plow the plains. A new millennium bows to the microchip!"

"You'll need more than chairs, ma'am. It's dark in here, bound to get darker still, and for your work – "

Mock on, like every bullying needy male! God or human, you need our subjection like a tonic, throw away the bottle. Scarf the spinach, Popeye, fling the can, wherever it falls somebody can be counted on to erect you a temple.

" – you'll need obscurity but not total darkness. The tripod's a nice touch, but couldn't you have asked me first before taking my last toke of tobacco?" He shuffled and scoffed, grinning hugely, as though he'd scored an enormous coup.

Danaid turned to me uncertainly. Was this big man my servant, consort, what? He was altogether too familiar, in both senses. He was too much like her husband. Well, of course! He had been that man, and he was as familiar on every one of the changing billboards. Was this the famous sense of humor? Bullying, no more!

"I'll buy you another sack, Ben, never fear."

"Thank you, ma'am. I'll go scrounge up some light. We're not fireflies to produce our own now, are we?"

He tipped his cap, winking at Danaid, who shrunk back against her drape. In waning light it was hard to distinguish her from the material, a dark purple, and I imagined her blood taking the opportunity to circulate among its folds.

The mountainous woman felt his power. Of course, she was here because he had brought her, this meeting of two women separated by millennia no accident, as a way to demonstrate eternal dominion over us. He enjoyed his freedom of movement, he had no problem with taking on whatever appearance pleased him in a hemisphere far from caves stinking of goat.

"He'll be back soon, won't he?" Danaid asked. I heard longing as well as fear. When I saw that I shed some scruples about selling her to him.

"What were some of the wedding gifts you

left behind?" I asked, remembering my own bargain sealed by the god's rank dishonesty when he so clouded my mind I neglected to ask for youth as well as immortality.

Sitting in my clumsy chair I had a sudden almost electrical jolt that kept me from digesting Danaid's answer: "A beautiful wedding ring, diamond pomegranates surrounded by golden laurel leaves," she whispered, eyes aglow with remembering.

"He (who? My bridegroom? She was probably wondering) gave me nothing but exile – from kin, time and myself," I managed to spit out, but this is what I thought: What if Danaid and I were not two women but parts of one whole, and the god was now giving us a chance to reunite? Danaid had the courage to flee, put up resistance, even sacrifice herself before she gave in, which the god had to have approved, because he sent her the seaman with a rowboat in which she made landfall despite every likelihood to the contrary. Well, I too made landfall in this American city, substituting subway for stench-filled cavern, though the tripod, its gnarled rough legs as hairy as the shanks of a goat, remains the same.

In the room that seemed to hold its breath, the silhouette of Danaid's fresh round pale face cut bravely through the gloom.

He had kept this part of myself back, secreted it somewhere, perhaps on his person – in his ear, thigh? How was it decided this was the time to bring her forth? Has it been like a minute of his time, eons of mine? What is god's time?

The electricity that coursed through me was galvanising triumph: he cared enough to create me anew in Danaid! He may never have forgiven me, but he never forgot me either, because both of us refused to be taken by him. Once broken, hymen is like the shattered glass underfoot at a wedding, refuse. It was savory bait to lure a god, but with afternoon's adventure yawning into night, he's off on a passing cloud. Even simpler, I tossed my head and denied him mostly because he wanted me so much.

"Oh, Danaid, in my case no nuptials like yours were even planned, it was going to be al fresco all the way," I laughed bitterly. "I refused him and I didn't run – that would have been fatal – I just sat down, like a heifer refusing the bull, a bitch the stud."

"Did he disgust you so much?"

"Not at all, I was mischievous and contrary, I merely wanted to tease him. I would have given in, but he was clearly cross, I knew who he was, and I had ambitions to be more than just an afternoon toss in the hay."

"What do you see in our future, Sibyl?"

I was startled by her use of my name, so long since someone had uttered those syllables.

I rolled to the tripod where the tobacco had burned to ash arranged in a pattern. Pretending to study it, I stirred with one sooty finger. "The time may have come to submit," I intoned judiciously.

She shrank back. She had not come this far to easily consent to the unlocking of her precious barrier. Ben, I thought, will be more forthcoming. No matter that he is the god, he is also at least a man.

How long was he standing there quietly in the shadows next to the door that he had soundlessly opened and passed through?

With agility and strength anyone would have thought beyond me, I snatched the girl and fumbled her to my lap. "Over here, Ben, there's someone who needs the experience of a living man."

He was on to her in a moment. A cry as of wounded doe issued forth almost more softly than my ears are able to make out. Was that because of my proclamation? "The time may have come to submit."

As he thrust, I imagined a sky split by lightning, followed by a flood of nourishing rain that washed away my age-accumulated dust and dirt through her loosened thighs, a cracked dam, the girl I was, split open like nutmeat.

I closed my eyes to savor the imminent end of long exile, tasting the dream-unencumbered sleep I had a right to expect.

"Must have been the strain walking up all those stairs carrying that kind of freight, ma'am. Should have rented a place with elevator."

Loosened thighs? No more than the axle of my chair. Cracked dam? A collapsed wheel. The god, tricked, cozened? Forget it!

The man carried Danaid like a fleshy feather, mother cat holding a babe between her teeth, moving it to safer ground. Danaid, or whatever her real name was, played the role for all it was worth, leaning into him, mewling kitten beseeching milk.

Was I to play mouse to all those claws and teeth?

What a neat way to topple me from my accustomed perch on higher moral ground! A matter of timing, of which he was master.

He swashed noisily into the kitchen, throttled the tap, which vibrated and gurgled mortally, and filled a glass, which he held reproachfully up to light washing in from the billboard, demonstrating sparkling points of rust in solution.

To my eyes drowning in tears it looked like gold.

"Mica," he said, "fools' gold, gamblers' gold."

"You mean me, of course?" I snuffled (would he buy another tyke act?).

"That girl's sick, ma'am. She could die. It's possible. You don't want a dead girl cluttering up your new apartment?"

"You won't let her die," I said flatly, noting the appearance of an extravagance of candles placed judiciously around the place that lit up the stark bare walls with their water marks like stalactites and gave the room the atmosphere of a ruined cathedral.

In the corner Danaid was coming to herself. I lacked the energy to go to her, to keep up appearances, I just kept sitting in my crazily tilted wheelchair, beside which Ben hummed tunelessly while he busied himself instituting makeshift repairs.

"Why did you do that?" came a harsh cracked voice from a shapeless mass only a little thicker than the shadows. "Is my virginity worthless?"

"Don't you know yet what a burden it can be!" I choked out, my voice trembling with a passion I didn't know was still mine. "For as long as I've guarded my tattered band of flesh the joke's been on me, because while I had the thing, what Apollo really wanted was far from me."

A tense stirring in the corner told me I held her attention. Crazy, I spoke as though Ben were not in the same room. He was quiet, and if he knew what I was talking about he certainly didn't show it.

"You may as well know, both of you," I went on. "I was haughty the way people are who stand on shaky ground. Why didn't the god use his famous double sight to look through me?" I asked of neither in particular, "then he'd leave me alone, a shabby thing, in truth longing to be bedded, but not by him."

Ben remarked as casually as if he hadn't heard a word, "Lady, I can try to fix that contraption if you'll get out of it for awhile."

My throat choked with panic. Once out of my chair I was helpless against him.

"How's about sitting on your bed for a spell?"

He waited patiently to no avail. Neither of us could speak.

"Maybe you ladies could even figure with a little lie-down?"

I saw his strategy!

We didn't move, his honeyed words an alluring trap, easier to fall into than ever again to get purchase enough on its slippery slopes to climb out.

Then Danaid: "Is it the nature of your business to lure women up here for men to rape?"

What scorn and choked rage lived side by side

in that voice, issuing from a mouth as dark as the entrance to a sibyl's cave.

She hadn't understood my words as the beginnings of a confession.

"Never before, Danaid, and also not this time. I thought, on my lap, through you to me, it would... I know I sound like a lunatic or worse. We've known one another for only a few minutes, but I feel we are joined somehow, and if Ben... If Ben is... who I think he is... then your husband won't come looking for you, he won't find you, because he won't smell that... certain..."

Sullen silence flung my words back on me where they fastened like stinging nettles.

My wheelchair had come to rest directly in front of the window. Full night now. The mass of people writhing in and out of the mouth of the subway had become a pied thick black water snake with no beginning or end. With no head or tail to define limits, it was eternal. Horrible to see it free to own the night world, I felt at least I could fling something to make it lash out and disappear in a paroxysm of startle, not fear – too big for fear. Was this eater of the world anything but the python that Apollo killed while still in his cradle?

On this cue, a cradle appeared on the billboard, a graybeard rock-rocking it while peering fatuously inside, his other hand rhythmically repeating disappeared inside the cradle, perhaps fondling the invisible occupant, and with each thrust of his hand, the legend burst out in words like fat drops: "Most Absorbent! Dry Baby Equals Happy Baby!"

The old man turned to give me a clear view of his face, my father's face! Complete to the cracked lips I have longed to kiss and soothe these many years, but the hand that emerged from the cradle thrust in my direction a bloody lump – heart, or...?

A sudden cramp doubled me up. In the corner, Danaid was also doubled up – with laughter.

"Not such a bad place after all. Instant punishment for naughty behavior. Like when I was a child. You always knew where you were."

"A good childhood," I wheezed. "Yes! I had that too, even blissful," I lied, as another more severe cramp gripped my guts like pincers and peeled my wet bottom from the seat onto the floor, where I lay, continuing to project that false picture before my eyes, dully aware that each avowal only brought renewed pain. "My father loved me only as a father ought to love daughter," I grunted proudly.

Danaid, no slow study: "Then why does a tsunami force you to batten down the hatches every time you mention him?"

Even in agony I noted that her speech had a tang of the nautical, result probably of her extended exposure to voyaging.

Not sea breezes was the smell spreading through the room, but the acrid oozing contents of my bowels.

"Ben, please come help me."

Despite his bulk, he moved swiftly. A pungency of bitter almond stirred the air, almost overcoming the smell of sick. I imagined his carrying long spiny laurel leaves into the grove to be purified after the long fight with Python.

Like a child I held out both arms from which the material fell away, allowing an ancient munginess to well from my armpits. The process of my ageing was ever accelerating. If the god had something he wished for me to do he was well advised to get on with it in the race with dissolution! For me there would be bestowed neither laurel wreath at the end, nor transformation into tree or shrub – only dust.

"This will be part of your job, Ben. When too much spirit bashes around my insides and I fall." I tried to make my voice sepulchral as befitted the oracle, willing the gusts of nausea to depart from me. Evidently I was undergoing within my body Danaid's storm at sea.

"Whew! You'd better have him hose you off

and hang you up to dry!" Danaid blew out her breath contemptuously.

Up to dry. How she saw me: a desiccated sack of shit. Not far from the mark. My father had reached deep within (me, not just the baby carriage), pulled me inside out, and, lo and behold! What had been blushing peach shriveled to prune, globed grape to wizened raisin, leaving me to croak out my story in a voice that was a life-long death rattle.

His hands around me like those of a practiced male nurse, intimate but not suggestive, Ben carried me to the bathroom, which without my notice he had fitted with towels and soaps. A block of incense burned steadily, cutting through the miasma that surrounded me.

Beyond resistance, I gave myself up to his touch. What was the good of fighting? I had more to worry about than Ben, with spiteful Danaid in the next room, who had been summoned and decorated then discarded like packaging.

"What kind of prize do I make?" I asked weakly as Ben's smooth lower arm floated me in the scented water, while he gently held the sponge, rinsing foulness from everywhere with blunt clean fingers.

For a moment, as his sponge reached between my legs, I grew dizzy – with desire or terror?

From the bathroom window my father (it had to be my father) continued to probe into the carriage, his face pious as ever. Nobody could ever dream what he was doing to the helpless little girl inside.

"You have taught me what I never wanted to remember," I said sleepily, despite myself relaxed and with a certain peace I never knew before, feeling cleansed, realizing the infant that was me had early on begun to harden herself against the world that probed and hurt her.

"I worked an old folks' home. A lot of them died all at once. The bosses needed someone to take the heat. That's when I did the jail time."

I could see him. With the same blunt gentle hand, submerging one old one after another, sending them to the other side without pain. Not a bad way to go. Now my turn. Danaid. The ferocious dog that guards the gates in another form? Someone the god needs to do his hatchet job?

If only the god had come in Ben's form the first time around! He could have gentled me, a wild mare used to picking the freshest flowers and grasses in a field unfenced for as far as eye can see. If I could have been that mare, a real mare, meeting a stallion in the trees, his fierce, smoldering-but-liquid eyes on me his quarry, but appropriate, and then the foals! Oh, the foals I could have had, taking their fill of me while I stood proudly in sunshine, no need to shade my eyes as the god swung round the sky in his golden chariot, gazing at me with admiration from all sides before finally dipping below the horizon, leaving me to the soft gathering dusk, and to the nuzzling lip-smacking, then dozing, only to awake on my feet the next day to the chariot coming by again, certain, inevitable. Growing old that way, surrounded by my strong foals grown stallions and mares around me at the end, nosing me with their soft breath when I lay down for the last time.

From the other room, a strident voice: "I came for a reading. Am I going to get it?"

The soap slipped from Ben's hand and slid beneath me. I held my breath waiting to see how he would manage. But with his by-now usual dignity, he held me up, grasping the soap without the slightest disrespect. Apparently he had no present plan to smother me in the bathtub.

Before I found my voice, Ben answered for me: "She'll be ready in just a minute. She's just finishing the purification ceremony, OK?"

As I arose, Ben holding my elbow, I did feel purified, as though a chipped bathtub squatting on four grimy bird's claws in a shabby room with peeling paint, all I could afford, had been transformed into mother-of-pearl with swan fixtures running with centaur milk.

My empty breasts swung free as I put one foot after another over the side, but that did not take his attention, nor did he look at my scrawny belly whose pendulous flesh nearly hid my sex, since most of the lush hair that once flourished there has been long-since worn away by the tight robes I always wear.

"A kind of cocoon meant to keep the butterfly from tumbling out too soon?" Ben rumbled as he swaddled me in a clean bathrobe he found rummaging in my suitcases.

I flashed a look of gratitude at his forbearance. "I am only an old woman making a living," I said, but my heart was pounding as I ran over what he had said about jail for the death of many old people, mainly women, I suspect, the next one of which could well be me. Not really a bad way to go, smothered by a strong man, nothing personal, doing a duty. Given him to do by whom or what? Or was he just crazy? Like me.

Nevertheless, I was here to do a job, and Danaid was patiently waiting. Whatever did she think when I grabbed her? All part of the scenario? Maybe. She had been through so much, it may not have seemed outlandish. Curiosity can smooth over lots.

I tottered with what dignity I could into the other room and took my place. By now the candles were guttering, which only added to the effect.

Ben put more of his strong tobacco on the tripod and handed me a taper to light. I put my face into the fumes, which rose around me like a smoky embrace, flowing into my ears, mouth and nose. My eyes burned and even closed I saw glittering shards cutting into my eyeballs.

Terror shook me: would I ever see again?

Another kind of force possessed my limbs, I looked down as my skinny shanks covered themselves in coarse hair – goat, acrid goat smell filled my nostrils, crowding out the smoke.

The field of green I had seen before with horses was now populated with centaurs swerving and veering as they shot frantically in all directions with bows and arrows while the invisible god coolly picked them off one by one. As they crumpled, proud masculine trunks and heads no longer aloft, their female parts, usually hidden, spread for all to see.

In death is no dignity, I cried silently.

"Danaid, what is your real purpose? Why have you come? Don't you realize how dangerous I am to your very existence?"

She said not a word, but bowed her head, apparently eager to begin, unabashed by my essential nakedness under the robe, the smell of me – goat mixed with attar of roses soap – or Ben's presence, completely natural to her, apparently used to servitors of various stripes ready and eager to be of service.

Was she a queen in disguise, her story to me a dissimulation, flung into exile, reduced to poverty on account of some rival suborning her place? Perhaps she was thrown out for barrenness, unable to produce an heir to secure both their places in a pantheon far away, perhaps not even of this time or place?

I laid hands like dirty paws on her head, dug in, searching for what I knew not what, and then with all my might suddenly sliced my hand downward like a knife.

Her skull split right open as a melon does. Before her seeds had a chance to fall I had a vision of the memories each of them contained.

"Too fast," I cried, "slow it down."

Ben smiled, unaware of what was happening or having caused it not giving anything away.

It did slow down, until the seeds in air were no more than motes of fireflies as the god led me back from the woods toward my anxious sisters who had been calling like whip-poor-wills keening high and low after a mate.

"They're less worried about me than what will happen to them if they lose me." I could laugh now that I was no longer afraid of abduction or worse from the stranger who held my elbow in such a soft strong hand who had spoken to me urgently, of what I had no memory though it had been no more than a few minutes. But if I could not remember words, the music of his voice had been strangely wistful, kept apart, a butterfly thudding softly on the window.

He led me, but as he was not of this place and time, though he keenly desired it, and he melted away even as I saw my sisters and ran pell-mell to join them, relishing the change in their voices to scolding, happy to roll in their minty breaths.

This was but one of the seeds!

In Danaid's head, memory of my girlish abandon?

Another seed, another day. A still sterile world, my father's goats and sheep lying miserable in their loose coats, like victims of wasting disease. Gaunt and pale my sisters' cheeks, accusing their eyes, as I attempted to garland them in the selfsame field. Impatiently, they waved me away. I sat nearby, sulking, still plump. It finally came to me how altered they were, and the kine, and the landscape – a dry, brown, sterile rattling wind kneeing brittle branches to the ground with a rustling like skeletons rolled like tumbleweeds.

"Why is this thing, sisters?"

"You," they rasped, no voices left to them, their

throats too dry even to hurl accusations. "Because you wouldn't stay with him as you were meant. This is why we are dying. All on account of you. You don't even remember. You never do. And so we will die. Because you are selfish."

I was too tired and shocked to stop one more seed. Yet I knew they were not lost in dust but securely lodged within me, able to incandesce whenever I sat quietly, spinning or stirring the smoke, tirelessly ready to murmur against me.

The billboard now advertised hair straightener, a black woman being helped out of an expensive sports car, hair whipping off her shoulders like a living shawl, flashing the eagerly smiling man a luminous leg, his mere touch exciting her eggs into an incandescence illustrated by the electrified glow in her abdomen that went on and off like a heartbeat.

"That woman is nothing but a walking egg-sac, but then I was no more than a machine to produce prophecies for the god to clip like supermarket coupons," I said, fingers splayed in patient Danaid's thick oily hair. Her time at sea had imparted a fishy quality to her. I fully expected another illusion, Danaid gotten up as a flying fish hurling out the window to horrify me, yet more punishment from the god, for what? Because he was spurned. Over eons – enough.

Danaid a fish, her hair was kelp, pearly scales undulated on her flanks. How wonderful the transformation, from a girl rolling in fat to comely maid of the sea, altogether an improvement – I saw agreement in Ben's eyes.

"Now I'd better get her to the bathtub too, ma'am. Sometime, maybe you'll show me how to do that trick?"

Hoisting her over his shoulder, Ben did not neglect to run his hands over her buttocks and hairy parts. She squirmed but did not cry out. What kinds of sounds do distressed mermaids make?

"She's no more than a distraction, Ben, toss her in and get back here. We need to talk."

"Yes, ma'am. One more question."

"What is it now?" I replied, exasperated, not able to read his face.

"Does this kind live in hot water or cold?"

As I shot him a baleful look, he snorted and gave me a sly-fox grin over his shoulder while he shuffled off.

I looked after him in a quandary. "Shuffled off." Ben was certainly older than I first took him for. It was clearly hard work for him to carry Danaid over his shoulder, even with her diminished bulk since she entered my domain, if I may dignify a cheap cold-water flat in the polis as "domain."

As I rolled to where I could watch him, he tried to hide the years' increasing acceleration while he decanted Danaid with movements that would have been effortless minutes before into the tub, and I wondered if she was going to complain about being forced to swim in second-hand bath water.

If she was in any position to complain.

Ben sat abruptly, unrolling as he slid down the curving wall of the bathtub, head bowed to his chest. I gave a little cry in my throat, which caused him to raise his head with what looked to me like pain.

Another seed dropped. Or it didn't, and I saw with my eyes, not the eyes of history spread like gold to airy thinness beat over eons, a precious but cold lifeless hand programmed to snatch me from here-and-now to then-and-there.

Yes, the living sibyl saw a noble man suffering the onslaughts of time that cut into his flesh like multiple tiny scythes, or year after year of sluicing rain digging runnels into flesh unable to resist.

He looked steadily at me, not without humor on his lips that were dry and cracking.

Before I could call out to him, a little voice cleared its throat and commenced to mock. "The metaphors that occur to you are hard-wired, dear. The lips are indeed like parched river bottom, brow noble as the over-arching cliff, his hands outstretched are like unto supplicating branches reaching out to you, beseeching. And so on. Beware the trap."

And went silent. I froze, stock-still. Ben's hands trembled in his lap. I so wanted to snatch and press them to my own lips to soothe away their reddened chapped skin, kiss that cheek glossy with tears (or splashed dirty bath water).

A trap. A trick. Perhaps he had actually warned me of being about to show me one of his own, Amazing Eon-Ageing-In-Minutes, ending in a skeleton, the death of a god, all because one snit of a girl refuses her destiny. Refused her destiny. Same thing isn't it?

My father's eager trembling hand slicing at my little rosebud. I am in the carriage on the billboard. His huge wet mouth above looms close. I feel hot spittle on my nose and cheeks, foul odors rising.

"Oho, my little girl likes that, the darling. There's more where that came from. You'll see."

And so I did! Became a seer! For others, never for myself!

Refuse – nay – kill all bridegrooms!

One after another they came after me and it wasn't enough for me to turn them away with a simple negative, I ranged deeply into each of their shortcomings (some were short indeed), and they reeled away from me unbearable in their own eyes, ready only for oblivion; to try to persuade some other virgin of the wholesomeness of their seed was utterly out of the question. Tumbled into their tombs, every one of them. With my father smirking like a gargoyle while pretending to be troubled, even grief-stricken, over the waste of all those young men.

Hypocrite! How I would like to have him in my hands now, crush his bones, starting with his defiling hands.

"That's why you sent me Danaid, isn't it, Ben?"

Full of his pain I flew to him my words, hoping they had power to soothe.

"Because she killed her husbands, and she wanted to escape the one she finally shipped with to spare him certain death at her hands. She cared too much for him to allow it. Let him hate her but not despise himself. She sacrificed herself, nearly, to allow him to survive. Does he know about his close call? Or were you all the dramatis personae in that tableau, Ben? I wouldn't mind if you were. A parable is better than a metaphor, it moves to action as mere literature can't.

"Yes, now I am ready to adore you as Lord,

Ben. Just get up. Stop your descent on that ladder that leads rung by rung into the abyss. Where I cannot follow. I do not have the power. Even back then I did not possess such power. Oh, Ben, please."

I threw myself out of the chair on to the floor, fortunate that it retained a thin scrum of soap so that I slid right into his lap, where I laid my head, gushing tears I didn't know I had the moisture to exude.

I waited for the touch of his hand on my hair. If only it came I silently promised him that any goat-stinking cave he chose for me I would gladly infest, as well as endure with equanimity his philandering, because that is what gods do. Eternally fertile and becoming.

Just let his hand like rain descend on my parched plain, I pleaded silently, forgetting recent contempt for metaphor. It's all I have. What do I know? I shrugged. Only the godly recite their own deeds in parable form. Not me. I am not a god.

"But he promised to make you one, once, don't you remember? Don't let him take it back. Remind him, you great ninny!"

"I want nothing for myself, Ben," I said loudly, to overpower the voice clawing my throat like a dry cough, not daring to turn to look up at him.

What did I expect – towering cyclone, burning bush, the three-headed dog of hell?

But it was only Ben, shaking his tousled curly head. I could not prevent the thought: Do gods never comb their hair?

He laughed, privy to all my thoughts, as intimate with them as he had been between my thighs with the sponge.

I drew back. Was this no more than a charade, a trick I played on myself, Ben no more than a roustabout ex-con on parole for the serial murder of old women warehoused in the place called 'convalescent hospital'?

"Good try, Ben, but I was never the virgin you took me for."

"A terrific trick, ma'am. I've never seen the like," Ben piped, his voice thin and reedy, "and here's me getting older at the same time as you going back. Quite the young thing as you are, I wouldn't be surprised if you jumped up and kicked that contraption out of your way and went after the billboard, since you hate it so much."

With "there's more where that came from" booming in my ears like the echo of an echo of thunder, I squirmed, impaled on his fingers like a soldier speared but not dead soon enough to be spared seeing and feeling the horrible point protruding from his shoulder blades.

I could be a blade, captive these many years in the guts of the monster, finally breaking free into the air, breathing again, casting off confusion.

I could be a spear.

But there was no way to the billboard except down the two flights of stairs, out onto the boulevard, across a busy street, and even then I didn't know if there was any way up to the sign when and if I got there.

"You don't intend to make it easy, do you?" I smiled fondly, trusting at last – such a good feeling!

"Bon voyage," Ben said.

I would swim across! Stroke my way against the hostile currents until, defeated, they consented to carry me to the sign, swelling no less than the shrill pan pipes I heard beginning to make their triumphal procession to meet me, the bride.

Around and around the staircase. Once, taking a breath, I looked up and there was Danaid, slim and radiant, waving me on.

A crowd gathered quickly, pointing up at the old lady making her way up the ladder to the illuminated billboard. Someone had maliciously greased the skids, and more than once I clutched the side rails to keep myself from being dashed on the street below.

I heard sirens, obscuring the panpipes. “Be still, you fools, this music is for me!”

Below were all manner of red vehicles. I shook away tears of joy that filled my eyes. I had to see!

Yes, there they were, in the window of the apartment. I shouted: “It’s high time for you to wed, you two, don’t delay, hear?”

If they did hear, they gave no indication, only nodded encouragement. Well, that would have to do.

He had lent me his story, the god – what greater devotion could there be?

As I clambered over the side of the baby carriage and fell inside, I barely had time to turn myself around when the huge face loomed, the warty wet hand lunged and the pythia took hold of the serpent and dragged him into the carriage.

His frightened face, now no bigger than my own, faced my grim eyes. He did not deserve a word from me. I took his neck and wrung it like a chicken and indeed it was as scrawny.

I heard the collective gasp when I flung it reeking and trailing cords, a glazed expression of horror still on it, into the street. When I raised myself to look over the side, it had rolled, herding the crowd before it, into a gutter.

An explosion of fireworks made me look up.

The sign was flinging great points of light into the air, and the legend –

Was putting itself together too slowly for me, a great clean emptiness in my gut where the ball of dirt had clotted all my years, for so long I never knew I could be so light.

Trust! I was the god in his cradle strangling the serpent. This gift!

Now I would go to him. Of course they cried, "don't jump!"

But I only leapt into my true life.

# LEROY

He mumbled an apology to the homeless person who sat or sprawled at his usual station outside the market where Leroy bought his orange juice. The man peered out from under bushy eyebrows, a hooded look that could have meant anything, but probably meant that he remembered Leroy and expected a dollar. Leroy reluctantly pulled out his frayed wallet and extracted a dollar. The man didn't deign to offer thanks, but Leroy hurried on anyway, intent on remembering the list he had forgotten, and about which his wife would purse her lips. She wouldn't say anything. She didn't, anymore, now that she was convinced that Leroy was losing it. He had to agree, kind of. It was almost pleasant not to feel responsible for a full bushel. Whenever he was successful nowadays it was a victory. Deep down, however, he knew it was a cop-out and he was as vital and alive as he had ever been. A secret he kept close to his chest.

The basket was unduly hard to separate from its mate. Leroy imagined that the two of them had a thing going that mere humans wouldn't understand. Leroy, however, was not one of the herd. He sympathized with their doomed relationship, separated just when overnight they realized their affinity for each other, their desperate need to remain together, not to be wrenched away to carry miscellaneous products, soon to be translated into garbage. Leroy pondered whether he might be able to navigate the two of them together. Before he came to any valid conclusion, someone else barged ahead of him, impatient to get it over with, and with a not-so-mighty tug, pulled them apart. Leroy, left with the one remaining, signaled his whole-hearted commiseration, and entered the store, careful not to speak his secret out loud.

The cart had one irregular wheel, but rather than substitute it for another, Leroy was careful to keep it on a regular path, knowing that if he relegated it to an unused bunch, it might in turn be relegated to a junk heap, to be buried under tons of other unwanted outmoded items from this dispensation, this planet.

As Leroy passed in front of the counter with heaps of un-organic bananas, he noticed a quite tall, not-so young woman looking at him. Another, not so tall, stood near her, fingering cucumbers. "Hello," the tall one said, "I noticed your beautiful sweater. Is it cashmere? May I feel it?"

"Why not?" Leroy answered, with a grimace, his usual facial furniture when he wasn't sure of something that was happening.

"Purple suits you well," this angular lady said brightly. "Do you hail from here?"

"No," Leroy answered, "San Joaquin Valley is where I was hatched. You probably were born somewhere cold, like Canada." He thought that was kind of witty.

"Ottawa," she answered, looking amazed, "how did you know?"

"I kind of do that sometimes," Leroy answered modestly, "I kind of read people's minds. Doesn't work with horses, though," he said and laughed, a little too loudly, so he coughed to cover it.

The tall woman lingered feeling the texture of the sweater, her hand moving over it in a way that Leroy imagined was kind of sensual, unusual, forward, near his chest, and the other lady chortled. His angular one turned to her and said to Leroy, "My friend there doesn't take to strangers. She's kind of a hermit crab. Mostly just a crab," she said, taking her hand away, to Leroy's disappointment, and laughed. The other lady put down the cucumber without any kind of expression and began examining a navel orange.

"My name happens to be Ottawa," the tall one said. "Quite a coincidence, wouldn't you say? Actually, not, my mother didn't have a lot of imagination."

Leroy remembered his list of items. "Nice meeting you, Ottawa, and what's-her-name too," and began to move off.

"Wait," Ottawa said imperiously, "I've got to have a hug," and moved toward him. Obligingly, Leroy stepped forward and trod on one of her feet. Which embarrassed him. He muttered an apology.

"Don't worry, I've had worse. See you later," she called out, waved and trundled her carrier toward the eggs, where her friend was already examining one with intensity. What could be so interesting about eggs? Particularly jumbo. What did he need. Yes! Orange juice. Did orange go well with purple? What kind of thought was that, he pondered. The lights in the place seemed brighter than usual, the people milling about even more peculiar than usual. Of course, this was a market in a hippy part of town. Hippy? Nobody uses that term anymore. Well, what are they, then, young mothers and fathers with infants strapped to their fronts, in serious conference with their mates in front of the cheeses? Many bearded ones, not like the homeless outside the shop, but brisk, knowing what they want. Leroy had a pang, remembering his own youthful self which hadn't been at all like these men. He had been painfully shy.

Never would he have dared to speak to a complete stranger in a market. He met his wife, Belle, in the stacks of a library, and only after many times did he dare ask her if she needed help in reaching down a volume.

He had looked at the title. Asimov. Science fiction. "Do you like science fiction?" he gasped.

"Oh, yes, very much," she replied, also blushing. Both of them virgins. They almost advertised it on their sleeves. But it hadn't been true. She'd had a report to make. It was an assignment.How disappointed he was when she told him, as she had to, her confession. He had retained his interest over the years. She had only ever tolerated it. Her taste ran to historical novels featuring decapitated queens.

Here, these strange people in the market could be a congeries of aliens. He liked to think so. Maybe he would be selected and elected to join them if he showed himself eager and ready, not at all affected by all those stories of anal probing. What would they want with his anus, anyway? he explained inside his head.

What would he ask for? He knew he mixed up fairy tales with alien incursions, but what the hell, why not? He would ask for several inches in height. Disappointingly, he had shrunk over the years. Spinal cord tightening, the things between the bones shrinking. What are they called?

"Vertebrae," he was sure he heard someone pressing a finger into a loaf of bread say.

"What?" Leroy asked, halting his cart.

"Did you speak?"

The man unbent himself. "No, man, I didn't."

Leroy, the so-called "man", waved his hand in apology. "I thought I heard you say, 'vertebrae,' and I was just trying to think of the word myself. That's all. No offense."

The man laughed, "At your age, what you need to think about is compression of your discs."

"Right," Leroy said, amazed, "that's what I've got, since I lost about two inches." Discs, he thought, yes, and what about flying saucers, discs in the sky. Right above the market, invisible, of course, waiting for a signal.

The man was gone. Leroy peered around but he was nowhere to be seen, disappeared around another aisle. Leroy felt inclined to follow him, just to see what he would do next but decided against it – too obvious that he wondered about the man's origins. He could be one of Them, coming out from behind his disguise inadvertently, showing his true self.

Were the managers of this place in on it, or was this place an innocent facility, chosen at random? Or because they knew that Leroy usually shopped here?

Ridiculous! Let's get the orange juice and vamoose out of here before I make a fool of myself, Leroy thought.

The woman, Ottawa, banged her cart into his. "Sorry, I lost my driver's license somewhere," she laughed, making light of it.

Leroy had to think that his cart probably flinched. He wanted to bend to apologize to it, but he realized he would make a fool of himself.

"Some people are just more sensitive than others," Ottawa announced seriously, half to her companion, and half to Leroy, so that he couldn't be sure she really meant the comment for him. "I forgot to get yours, Mr. Nice Sweater."

"Leroy," Leroy answered, a little nervous at this re-meeting. He wondered if she was a kind of con artist, after older men, an easier catch than the men with babies on their chests.

"Leroy," she breathed, "I might have guessed. 'The king,' it means. It means you are a king. Did you know that, Leroy, the king?"

"Of course I know the origin of the name," he huffed, somewhat put off, a little alarmed. The noise level of the market seemed markedly increased, or embarrassment was increasing his sense of a kind of oppressive atmosphere he had never noticed before.

"The king," her companion huffed. "Sure.

You meet them every day in the canned corn."

Leroy turned to her with some dignity. "I never claimed anything."

"Well, there are plenty out there who just might do it for you," she retorted and turned to the yoghurt, looking closely at the label for the Greek kind.

Very strange behavior, Leroy thought, now anxious to get away. "Well, the orange juice is awaiting me with baited breath," he laughed.

The man from the bread section wheeled by, muttering again, this time, something like "he's too little. He needs to be bigger. Stretched. Leave his bottom alone, though."

Now, Leroy thought, I'm truly imagining things. Nobody, but nobody would say that.

Just then, to his utter surprise, Leroy noticed the scruffy homeless man from outside scrunched into one of the carts. He was picking items from here and there, being pushed by a very large man, maybe a wrestler, with massive biceps and a shiny bald head, which seemed to radiate light and a kind of energy.

This couldn't be happening, Leroy thought. That man wouldn't be allowed in the store. Never. Dirty. Smelly. Certainly without money. But maybe not, he thought, thinking of his own dollar – and maybe lots more where that came from.

OK, let's say, just for fun, this is a meeting place for aliens, Leroy thought. I've been mistaken for a king in disguise. Maybe I am. Nobody knows his or her origins past a few generations. Maybe I'm an alien too, lost here, having forgotten my mission.

Leroy imagined he heard a murmur from his cart. It could only be the thumping and squealing wheel. I'm not up for a talking market cart, he thought.

From the next aisle he heard Ottawa's voice. The only way he could hear it would be if she were actually shouting. Or if she was speaking inside his head in a mysterious way. No, forget that. He hurried on to the refrigerated unit where the orange juice was kept. He looked up and down for their favorite, the kind of juice with lots of pulp. Strange, there was every other kind, but the slot for his kind was absent.

"Are you looking for this?" a now-familiar voice queried.

Leroy didn't want to look around. The hair on his neck rose. If he had any hair left on his head he was sure it would have risen like in horror stories. "Yes, I am. Why do you know that? Look, you are kind of strange. You're kind of entering my fantasies. Yes, I would love to be taller. If you're from another planet, yes, I'd like to go there with you.

Take me away," Leroy said, in a comical kind of voice, in case she was just a masher out for a good laugh at his expense.

He turned to face her, aware that he was looking at her very much the way the homeless man had looked at him. And waited.

Ottawa didn't laugh in his face. Instead, she gently placed the orange juice with lots of orange bits in it in Leroy's basket. She didn't speak. The sound in the market had gone silent. As though the volume had been turned way down. From some central place. Maybe from the invisible ship hovering above. Leroy shivered in the sudden cold. Or his blood pressure had plummeted. He was dizzy. He thought he could faint. That would be bad. His insurance didn't cover ambulance. His wife would be very annoyed at the expense. But what if he was having a stroke, he mentally protested, justifying his dizziness to his absent wife, who brooked no nonsense about aliens in the market, particularly those who knew about pulp.

"Sit down, Leroy," Ottawa said kindly. "But we've got to go now, my friend and me. And we both wish you a long and happy life. Where you are. Now."

Leroy was too dizzy to ask if she was from another planet. Instead, as if inside his head he heard the other one say crossly, "I never thought the name meant anything. Or his imaginings. Your system's too sensitive. Try to tone it down next time. Let's go," she seemed to be saying, impatiently.

When Leroy allowed himself to be picked up by the manager, he retrieved his now-silent cart, went to the checkout and waited patiently, searching the store for the peculiar duo, but they were nowhere to be seen. Before he was altogether checked out, he came to realize he had somehow failed an important test, that he would never be chosen.

He walked his injured cart to the overly bright sunshine outside. The homeless man looked up. "Never mind, man, tomorrow's another day. Got any spare change?"

## SPARE CHANGE

LEROY — CHAPTER 2

There can be some arcane meaning in that phrase, "spare change." Spare means lacking in voluptua or even thin. Change means just what it says, change being something that can happen without volition.

Maybe particularly without volition. Maybe never, if willed. Still, Leroy sighed (his teachers had always complained that he sighed too much), to put this much weight on what a bum mutters, probably to everybody who passes, or at least to those he remembers have offered him a buck, is just plain silly.

The car didn't want to start. OK, that's absurd, Leroy reproved himself. I need to think: the car doesn't start. It doesn't have volition. It can't not want to start. But, hadn't he had a romantic image of the conjoined market carts, sad at their being violently torn apart by an uncaring customer? Absurd, of course, but kind of a diversion when he had to go on a boring trip to the market, only for orange juice. And bananas! Damn, but he forgot the bananas, mostly because of those pesky women. He still felt the impress of the tall one's hand on his chest. He looked down. Was there a depression there? Of course not, he shook his head at annoyance with himself. The main thing is to get the car going before the juice spoils.

He glanced out the window. The bum wasn't looking at him. Nothing strange there. Of course, he thought, I am trying to make things strange. I will not look up to see if the space ship is hovering there, visible only to me, maybe pulsing light in a kind of Morse code.

Sternly forbidding any silly movements, he began to open the driver's side door after unlatching the hood. Crack! Another car peeled some metal off the car door, leaving the rear vision mirror in pieces. The other car stopped after a hundred feet. More delays! The door was still working, though crimped, he saw. Leroy took out his phone to photograph her car. Before he spoke to her he noticed she was talking on her cell phone. Of course, the idiot was so busy on her phone she didn't see how close she had gotten to his car.

He took several pictures. She was agreeable to exchanging information. She drove off, still talking. What an idiot, Leroy thought. He got back into his car. He brought up the pictures.

Or tried to. There was the car. He recognized the scenery. The woman, though, was nowhere to be seen! She was out of the picture.

This is not possible, Leroy thought. Not here and now. How could this happen?

The car's motor came on. Leroy could not remember having succeeded in getting it to start. My mind is going, thought Leroy. Well, I'm older than when it usually starts, according to all the stats. I'm lucky I lasted this long. He thought of the exasperation his wife demonstrated when he forgot some simple request. She (what was her name, again? This was not funny, he thought) usually remembered herself and patted him on the arm or back and apologized for her short temper. Belle. Of course, Belle.

Leroy glanced at the bum. That is, he tried to glance at him, but he was gone. Leroy looked up and down the street. He was usually somewhere in sight, but he saw only another familiar, another homeless man, but entirely different from the one who was usually camped in front of the market.

Let's take stock, Leroy told himself sternly. I am deliberately causing myself to get into a weird place. Do I want to drive myself batty? Is this a way to get myself to finally retire from the stinky old school where I've been locked up for half a century? Then I've got to spend twenty-four hours a day with Belle, who, to be frank, is not as *bella* as she used to be, though she's aged pretty well – or at least not badly.

Well, now that the car's working, should I just go home or go back into the market for the bananas? Oh, how trifling and pitiful all this is! Of course, if I am truly a king somewhere in some dispensation, having forgotten my mission, lost my futuristic tools, it stands to reason that I have become the least of mortals from having been superior to mortals everywhere in every time and in every clime. It's actually poetic, he thought, with some pride and the immediate self-jeering. As though there were two men locked in mortal (and immortal) combat inside me. Not two hearts, alas, like Doctor Who, but only an invisible and undetectable alien-ness.

One way to get this silliness out of me is to get back in there and run down those two women. They are probably working for some organization that wants to prove some silly theory. I won't fall for it, he thought, buttressing himself mentally.

He checked behind (his rear view mirror was gone), cracked open the door, checked the meter, which had another twenty on it, and strode to the door. Brought up short. It was closed. He checked his watch. Nothing unusual, really. It was a few minutes past nine. Place closed at nine. He looked through the glass door. Nothing inside. Nobody cleaning up. All the lights on, but nobody there.

Well, how is that unusual, he asked himself. Nothing unusual, answered a bland voice inside his head, which was suspicious. Every market has to clean up and restock during closed hours. This market looked like a stage set.

Well, the other part of Leroy asked, maybe it actually *is* a stage set. One set up just for me? He was about to go around to the back, when his phone rang. The woman-less picture faded and Belle's face came on. "I've been waiting dinner for you, Leroy. What in the hell is keeping you?" She was in an irritated mood, Leroy saw, needing to be placated. "I've been having some car trouble, Belle. And some dame sideswiped me. I've got pictures of her car, but somehow not of her."

Leroy was explaining, but to his shock, Belle seemed more and more to resemble the offending and offensive woman, both in feature and in timber of voice. Shaken, Leroy mumbled more apologies, but he didn't hear what she said, because she hurriedly had departed the phone. Leroy was left with the sound of his own heart thudding in his ears.

If this market wasn't so convenient to his trips to and from school he would have decided not to be a customer anymore. Too weird. Well, not the supermarket itself, but he became too weird every time he came here. Every time? Wasn't this the first time? Could he be sure if it was, or was his memory now so spotty?

Another part of him, along with his heavily beating heart, was repeating: you've failed some important test. You have to find some way to redeem yourself. Find yourself. Re-invent yourself.

Leroy gunned the engine (specifically against the carmaker's suggestion), to show his independence of spirit. Headed home.

"I am Leroy," he said out loud, "and that's certainly enough. For now," he added, somewhat to his consternation.

## WARRIOR

LEROY — CHAPTER 3

These streets are all familiar, thought Leroy, metaphysically wrapping his arms around himself, to comfort. It's good to have a sense of humor, however residual, after the buffeting of a long lifetime of grim people and even grimmer happenings.

Like his youthful lunge toward Israel, whose tenth anniversary lured him with promises of graduate school without tuition all those years ago. He signed all sorts of papers, even one that stamped him as a son of Israel, a Hebrew without portfolio, he liked to joke. If he was captured by the Arabs, he used to continue to joke, he could pass as a Christian, uncircumcised.

Uncut. Like the pages of books in the past. If they were to be read they had to be mutilated. Isn't that like life? Once cut, the umbilicus continues to bleed throughout life. Sad, even crying, it wants its connection. Isn't that why I married Belle, he mused, the need for mother, though hidden, occluded by the need for sex?

"What a joke," he said out loud, narrowly missing a slow oldster on a crossing, who waved his stick at Leroy, who waved back apologetically, albeit insincerely. "I had a pang down there when that tall creature pummeled me on my chest." He touched the spot, reverently, always mocking himself for any errant thought that passed the blood barrier to his brain.

Belle was outside in the aviary feeding the birds when Leroy pulled into the driveway, which scattered squirrels waiting for their part. Leroy decided not to honk. Nevertheless, gravel crunched. One of the crested cockatoos showed alarm. Leroy could never get that bird's affection. Probably only liked females, he thought, not really sad, as it made him nervous sometimes when the bird would say something not parrot-like, but apposite, in relation to something Leroy was doing, like, filling a pipe, he said once: "Stupid. Shortens life. Bad experiment." That only partially made no sense, though, really, it all did.

She's like a bird herself, Leroy thought. Spreading her arms so that the little birds could settle on them, almost as though she could take wing herself. Alas, she was no longer quite so thin. Age has thickened her, Leroy thought. Nevertheless, there is something about her that is distinctly avian. In another life she might well have taken wing as a hawk, a red-tailed hawk, Leroy thought somewhat grimly, as they are quite able predators. Sometimes, she got so angry at Leroy that he thought she might peck at him. Bite him, he meant.

"The car wouldn't start," Leroy said, trying to preempt her irritation. He stood outside the aviary. So many birds. So much expense for birdseed, fruits, and vegetables. Of course, the lettuce for the turtles was free, he had only to scavenge behind the market for that, only having from time to time to deal with and fend off other dumpster-divers. It did give him a sense of the desperation of some of his species.

His species. Insofar as he was one of them, which he sometimes doubted, without much cause.

"Not to mention that stupid creature who bashed into my car and then disappeared. Damned phone." Maybe his anger, however feigned, would forestall any words from Belle.

"Your past has caught up with you," Belle said evenly.

"What do you mean?" Leroy replied with some alarm, hiding it with a jocular smile, indicating that he thought Belle was teasing him. A relief.

"You just got your induction notice from the Israeli army."

"I just got what?"

"There's a letter. And they called. It seems

you have skills that are needed. You signed a paper decades ago that promised you would always be available."

"I did?" Leroy said, astonished, trying to remember what he signed, what he promised. As he frantically combed his memory, items seemed to unroll in his mind. Was he really an automatic weapons expert, an innovator in robotics? A cool battlefield officer? He felt his chest. Yes, there was a depression there left over from urgent surgery, flack, pressure from an explosion that pushed in his armor.

There was a girl involved too, but she was more of a murmur, a shadow. Belle was looking at him as though she was in his life right now. Guiltily, Leroy looked back. Should he mention the strange women in the market? He suddenly remembered the orange juice in the trunk. "I got the orange juice," he called cheerily, disturbing a packet of parakeets, who scolded and reset themselves on Belle's head, making it look as though she had a crown of feathers.

"Well, are you going to heed the call of duty or are you going to make the excuse that you are too old for this sort of thing? They aren't at war, are they?"

Belle prided herself on not keeping current on world events. Her world was the birds, the turtles, sometimes volunteering at the local humane society. Certainly Leroy was glad that his job could pay for all the expenses, though he sometimes wondered how it did. He tried not to interfere in their financial life. Glad she took care of it.

Summer is coming, he thought. I'm not doing summer school. Should I go? Why not? And then, he remembered with a guilty thrill, I could look up Rena. If she's still alive. What can she be doing? Probably in an old-age home, he thought, with some distaste. Maybe where I should be. Where I will be if I lose it any more.

"If I promised, I have to do it. Though I'm sure they can't extradite me, can they?" Leroy laughed a little uneasily. Belle was taking this altogether too calmly. Was she up to something? Did she have – gasp – a lover? Leroy had to laugh.

"Have you ever thought how dangerous a man I am, really, Belle? Weapons expert. I can devise a robot that will keep you under surveillance at all times." He made a spooky face and raised his arms, unconsciously mimicking Belle's posture.

She looked at him without expression. Slowly, she unbirded her arms and walked through the double doors of the enclosure. She walked toward him, still without expression. Slowly, she put her arms around him. "I think it's really wonderful of you to care that much about your people."

Leroy, glad for her embrace, tried to find the words to explain, again, that these were not his people. In fact, he really didn't know who his people were, or if he had any. A moment of panic. How did he remember some things and not, important, others? Arbitrary. It was all arbitrary. Not orderly.

But Israel. An orderly place. With a definite beginning. Definite needs. Rena had definite needs. One of which was for him to join her in Israel, where she waited for him. Had he made promises to her? Well, going again, maybe he could find out, after all this time.

All what time?

## RENA

### LEROY — CHAPTER 4

It's already high summer in Israel, Leroy mused, picking through his closet and drawers for reasonable clothing. What for desert, what for city? The whole thing seemed unlikely, even impossible. Sure, he had offered some innovations to the armed forces. Maybe even helped push back the Syrians from the Golan. What was it? It was to laugh not remembering something so heavy, the sum of which felt like it was pushing him right now. He had to lie down. A force was on his chest. Is this the worried-about heart attack? Probably not. It was actually the letter in his breast pocket pressing down on him.

He was feeling guilty also of not minding leaving Belle alone, with her birds. She could take care of herself. He had to leave a will, of course. Just then, Belle sauntered into the room, fluttered a piece of paper, and left just as silently. How did he know that this piece of paper had to be a will? Of course, unsigned it had lain languishing in a drawer for many a year. She was not being weird, just practical, her usual self.

The date, the time, the place? Leroy barely had time to think about all these factors, when a loud whirring intruded on his questions. Belle came back. "Your horse just arrived," she said.

"My horse," Leroy repeated. "Of course. I've had many horses. Just how many I would have been able years past to tell you exactly, if you cared to know. Actually, do you?"

"No, dear," she said affably. "I'll hold them off until you finish packing."

A small cadre of uniformed men appeared in the bedroom, saying nothing. They exuded a mixed scent Leroy remembered: dust, crumbling ruins, decaying pages of innumerable bibles, anxious sweat, gunpowder. These men were composed of those things, Leroy thought; they weren't really separate entities. Did that mean that Belle was really a composite of her birds? Of her years with him? Would he be able to smell these things if he put his mind to it? Silly. Still.

"Are you expecting a war, you guys?" he said, just to start a conversation. "I need a few minutes." He expected some sort of reply but got none. He imagined their mouths were taped shut. He could almost see it. He wouldn't have been able to hear anything anyway, because of the roar of the helicopter. Something I should have given some attention to, he thought, before I left the country. Stealth copters, that's what the world needs. Still, that issue has been overtaken by drones, he recalled, with some chagrin. Losing it again. He sighed. They really, really don't need me.

Belle was outside chatting with the pilot. He didn't seem reticent, at least not with a woman, Leroy thought. One of the soldiers hefted his suitcase aboard. Another passed a kind of wand over him, evoking a strange buzzing sound. It felt as though his very interior was being probed. At least not anally, he chortled silently.

And then, the next thing he knew, they were aloft. Leroy was groggy. Had he been offered something to drink when he boarded? He couldn't recall. It seemed a long time since he had kissed Belle for so long. He looked out the window. Somehow, he could still make her out, waving, a swirl of birds around her declining form, waving until she disappeared as a speck.

The moment that happened, Leroy was aware of someone sitting beside him. Somehow he didn't want to turn his head. If he did, everything in his world would come to a screeching halt before heading off in another direction. Would that be so bad? It was already happening.

So he turned. A very crumpled figure sat there, the same ironic turn of the lips, albeit those lips were creased and covered over with wrinkles, and the wrinkles covered by a copious application of lipstick, whose odor Leroy instantly recalled, because he had carried it with him after their trysts for many a day. In fact, his compatriots at headquarters often chided him about it. His own lips blazed red even after scrubbing. She was still wearing the same brand, the same scent.

Rena.

"I won't ask what you're doing here, because I don't really know what I'm doing here. If this is all a dream. If I am floating in a sea of deception."

"You deceived me plenty, Leroy," Rena growled.

She often growled, Leroy remembered, usually in a loving way.

"I couldn't stay, Rena, you know that. I was on leave. I would have lost my job in the States." As he said that, he realized how ridiculous it would seem, to a woman who had given her heart and her body to the alien, him. She had always treated him as though he came from another dispensation, maybe another planet. Actually, with that in mind, he was able to devise machines from the bottom up, with no prior prejudices. She was very helpful, but alas! he had to betray her. Better to let that go.

"They gathered me up from the refuse pile just to remind you of what you can do for Israel," she said, in a disgruntled voice. "I'm out to pasture, like an old goat, but now they give me fresh meat and expect me to jolly you up like in the old days. Don't expect to see me naked."

"No, indeed," Leroy hastened to reply. "Never. I'm married, you know, or don't know. For a long time."

"Doesn't cut any ice," Rena retorted. "Didn't bother you the last time."

Of course. He had been married when he had his affair with Rena! Silly kind of excuse now. A half-century out of date, that excuse. Still. He wasn't going to manhandle that bag of bones sitting beside him, sipping on a martini as though she hadn't had one for centuries.

"But why you? After so long? To what purpose? There must be some real desperation, to haul me back in."

Rena appeared to him to be in better shape after she'd signaled for another martini, downed it and turned to him with a nicer look. In fact, she wasn't so bad after all this time. In fact, rather amazingly, she was very much like the Rena he had known all those years ago. "How have you kept your looks, Rena?" he said. "Really."

"Israel has made great strides in civilian cosmetic surgery, Leroy, although I wouldn't have been able to afford it for myself. Luckily, I knew you. I wouldn't ever have thought you would be responsible for my rehabilitation. So I'm as young as you can see. I don't know how long it will last. I'm a walking bomb."

"What?"

"You forget, Leroy, that I volunteered to do a Judith on the Syrian commander."

"What?"

"Oh, come on, I was beautiful, spoke impeccable Arabic, slipped over the border, into his tent, crept into his bed, and meant to blow us both up. But the damned thing didn't go off. I still have it, embedded in me. Who knows when it will blow? I don't. They paid me enough to go away and explode anonymously. Maybe now. Maybe then. Who knows?"

"This is fine," Leroy said indignantly, "and they plant you on me. What is this? A game of musical chairs?"

"Don't worry," Rena said, patting his hand, which caused Leroy to hastily pull it away, "the chances are it's a dud."

And, possibly, so am I, Leroy thought grimly.

# LEROY: MUSICAL CHAIR

## LEROY — CHAPTER 5

Rena, seated beside him, was like a dynamo whirling so fast as to become invisible. In fact, she faded as he did, because he couldn't keep his eyes open. She had always been dynamic, more than he could even bear. After spending a night with her he was always drained, in more than one way, heh-heh, he thought, unable to keep from making a joke of even the most important things.

But really: how so? It had been as though sleeping with Rena she pulled out of him all the experiences he had had since being with her last. And before. Long after he met her, he thought he could feel her dynamics crackling around him. Even in the here and now. He recalled a night after hiking in the desert, exactly where he didn't or couldn't remember. Exhausted, they found a shabby monastery whose cracked door Leroy had trouble opening. Ajar, it revealed a kind of fairyland of medieval faded splendor. Like a fairy tale, he remembered exclaiming. While Rena, more practical, shouted: "Is anybody here, for Christ's sake?" A little man, almost a gnome, with a hunchback, appeared as it seemed out of one of the mosaics, rubbing his hands together, perhaps with impatience, perhaps with nervousness. "Yes, in His name, what can we do for you? We're not used to guests. Aren't you covered with fine dust?" he asked, suddenly and surprisingly. Yes, they were. Leroy's armpits itched with accumulated sweat and grit. He longed for a shower. Rena abruptly said, "We desire lodgings, refreshment and whatever your obviously limited hospitality has to offer."

Leroy was appalled at her rudeness. But she whispered to him: "Underlings in this sort of place are used to harsh command. They only respond to it."

Leroy begged to differ, but what the hell, if it worked...

The little monk made motions for them to follow, abruptly stopped, faced them, troubled, features screwed as though ready to cry. Rena forestalled him. "Yes, yes, we're married. I have the document in my valise, but there's also underwear in there. Do you want to scavenge and roil and plunder with your dirty hands?"

"No, no," the little man hastened to say. "You are young, but that is what the new rulers want. More descendants of the original Semitic race. Perhaps you will begin to reproduce this very night, and report to your rulers of our hospitality."

Leroy hadn't been able to help looking astonished. This was a new kind of Semitism, off the charts, really. Or was it that?

They were introduced to a weir or sluice with running water, pure, cold, delicious enough to drink as well as bathe. The clouded dirty water ran off as though aware of its pollution, not wanting to stay another moment. Hidden bell-like instruments made the very atmosphere alive with sensual pleasure. How could something like this be within a desert monastery?

"It is their way of producing temptation to bodily pleasures," Rena explained with a look of distaste, which contrasted with her obvious joy in her own nakedness, having shucked off the grime of their day.

Leroy gazed at her with a mixture of animal desire and fear that she would suck from him the recollection of every single one of his experiences, which, after every one of their pairings, took on the feeling of long-ago faded memories. He was even afraid that if they continued to mate often he would be taken back to the womb and before, that he would cease to exist as an independent entity.

These feelings were so absurd he certainly couldn't share them with Rena. Still, he looked at her and felt that she knew without his ever saying a word.

That wasn't all. Mosquitos swarmed the ceiling of the little room they were given. Nothing did Leroy hate more than those damned biting things. He closed his eyes and their sound seemed to amplify. He buried his face in Rena's armpit, wishing to glory in the female scent of her skin; naturally perfumed, it seemed to his intoxicated senses. Also, she was kind enough to foreswear lipstick during this interim, for which he was grateful.

However, instead of the luxury of skin, he got renewed amplified buzzing. One or more of the damned creatures had sneaked in there too!

"Damn," he growled. But then the racket stopped. He plucked his head away and looked up. Nothing. They were gone.

"I never knew you were so bothered by them, Leroy," Rena said, either drowsy or languorous or both. She positioned herself for him. He wanted to discuss this miracle, but she hushed him with one fragrant finger. Was it always thus? Why, yes, it was. He wanted to ask her about it. Instead, she waved her finger like a magic wand, which caused him to become erect immediately, each time a bit more manly, another thing. It was certainly nice, but unnerving nonetheless. He shrugged and attributed the phenomenon to her amazing vigor, strength, casual ability to move things he would have thought immoveable.

Might as well plunge in, he thought, be happy you are so lucky. But then, as though his mind turned a corner and looked into another room, he thought of Belle, newly married, still carrying the blush of her virginal white lace gown and white roses, scentless, but lovely. In this place also resided guilt, hunkering in a corner, ready to pounce. But the figure of Rena, transparent as a dragonfly's wings, stood in front of the figure of Belle, quietly but firmly urging her into a closet, along with the figure of guilt, who resisted a bit, but finally fell victim to Rena's amazing charms.

All this as he was doing what he came to consider his job of work, pleasant as it was, resigned to losing yet more of his middle years. Sucked up, as it were, by Rena's amazing organ.

"This is the last time, Leroy," she'd said in a matter of fact tone, as though this statement couldn't matter less.

"What do you mean, Rena? Are you mad at me? Haven't we enjoyed ourselves? I mean, I have to get back to the kibbutz. There's an experiment I'm doing there that needs me, but we always have to break it off before we're ready, don't we?" He put on his most hangdog melancholy look.

Rena laughed, it seemed sincerely. "I'll tell

you a military secret, Leroy. I am about to become a living, walking bomb. To be implanted in me," she pointed down, "will be an explosive; when detonated, powerful enough to take out a city block or more. Because it hasn't been tested, they really don't know how big it will be. The brass are very interested."

Leroy looked bewildered. "You mean you're going to be a suicide bomber? You're going to willingly blow yourself up? Are you crazy!"

"It's what I was born for, Leroy," she said, matter of factly, as though discussing the weather. "You wouldn't begin to understand. Remotely."

"Try me," he yelled. Strangely relieved. Now he could leave the country with a clear conscience, no guilt. He could, little by little, tempt the memories of his life with Belle to return. He would be unable not to imagine Rena while having sex with Belle, but still. Perhaps all traces of guilt will disappear in time, he thought.

"You see, you're already getting used to the idea. But there's one thing."

"What?"

"You see, this thing is so new. I've been tested. After one of our rendezvous. The device can only go off when detonated by your chemistry."

"You mean..."

"Yes, that's what I mean, your product,

what you produce in copious amounts."

Leroy blushed a little, flattered. Then thought. "You mean we have to infiltrate together, find a place to lie down, make love (in that perilous situation he really meant, but didn't say, screw), and die?"

"For all the Jews of the world, Leroy."

"I'm not Jewish, damn it, Rena, I've told you over and over."

"Doesn't matter, Leroy. You are as one of the kings of ancient Israel, and I am another Judith, except I'm not after your head."

"This is a test, isn't it, Rena? You can't mean it. I mean, you're playing with my credulity."

Rena looked at her fingers. Leroy pulled back a little, dislodging some flaking plaster from the wall. It made a little hushing sound, as though to comfort him. "I don't want to do it, Rena. I'm not going to. You'll have to find someone else for this grisly caper."

"There's no timetable, Leroy. It isn't for now. When the time comes, you will know and you will be more agreeable. No force will be involved, no coercion."

Next day, when they returned to Tel Aviv back to the kibbutz, his experiment succeeded – a robotic device that rolled guided into the midst of the enemy, displayed its location on a remote video and exploded on cue. For which the brass presented him with a hush-hush medal, which he kept forever after in a small plush box at home.

Now here, once again, was Rena, drinking large amounts of alcohol, looking hardly a day older, and doubtless still carrying, like an unborn fatal child, the aggressive tumor of a bomb.

He chilled to think. Is this the long-delayed fuse ready to be lit? Could he even tell her he had been impotent for a very long time?

Luckily enough.

## LEROY: IMPOTENCE

LEROY — CHAPTER 6

How is he going to tell her, the very signifier of libido, that he is no longer able to penetrate her, scrape out the hidden gold of her interior, force her to cry hosanna to the skies?

Also, face it, he had a sneaking suspicion that her frenzy was mostly a put-on. Even then. Even when the affair was new. How did it start? The whole thing was bogus. He found her under one of the pillars of Ocean Park Fun Pier. He had been observing how his footsteps disturbed very small crustaceans, who scurried back into the safety of the sand after being disturbed. He pretended to hear them shout to each other about where the safest refuge might be. This happened over and over. He wondered if the small creatures were involved, if they forgot from one emergency to another what to do. If they had a central command, they would... And then he saw her, huddled over a small fire. Since it was one of those fiery southern California days he was puzzled at it.

"Excuse me, miss, but are you all right?" This in itself was unusual for Leroy, a solitary, brooding intellectual. That's how he thought of himself. Of course, the "intellectual" part was very hazy, as he hadn't yet found a subject.

"Look at the fire," the girl said without other greeting. "See how the smoke curls up as though it had been lost and is only now about to find its true home. I also need to find my true home, with the intellectual mate of my heart."

Such an unusual speech, even reiterating something of what he told himself so often. He looked more closely at the smoke. At that moment, into his mind came the impetus for one of the first of his epoch-making inventions. He later found a way to harness smoke to be able to predict weather, wind currents, the stock market, and various other less sensational uses. All coming from his chance meeting with the girl, who turned out to be Rena.

The very progress of their affair was foretold in those first few minutes.

"Let me warn you, nameless attractive man, I demand all of your attention, or none. I will disappear into the smoke, as it dissipates, unless you can come up with the magic words to keep me here, in your dispensation."

Leroy laughed uneasily. So much drama! He decided to play along with it. "What if I don't have the necessary male stamina to keep you here?" An obvious reference to the fact that his testicles had not descended until his sophomore year in college, and that lacking certain hormones predicted a less-than-average masculinity.

Rena turned to face him face-on. She smiled warmly. "None of that is as important as that you become my life-long power source."

Leroy imagined that the top of his head, prematurely bald, started to shine as though it were a dynamo. He had to laugh.

"Yes," Rena said seriously, "I can see it. I can feel it." She held out a delicate blue-veined hand, which, even through the reek of seaweed and a strong whiff of urine, smelled of exotic perfume. Leroy, after a little hesitation, took it, feeling that this girl was probably crazy and he ought to just go on squishing tiny crustaceans.

Still, he took the hand and everything after, always being somewhat diffident about asking about how she happened to be just where he was on that late afternoon.

And the ecstatic lovemaking directly under the roller coaster, which rumbled with huge vibration as they both climaxed. Best not to ask.

She found him a prize ticket to Israel, and his innovations were lauded by the brass, and he found himself living in a communal farm, a kibbutz, making life easier with improvements to tractors, milking implements, fertilizers. He had to be removed from the kibbutz because of the sore irritation he caused all the other thinkers.

But then came the bomb. Both the statement of it and the thing itself.

The chronology gets very mixed up here. Those in charge were very careless, because to them it made no difference, there being no separation by the present of the past and the future. Leroy was as the crustaceans were to him, anonymous, multiple, replaceable.

No! All that was part and parcel of his fantasy past. The life he was living was life. Was life. Is life.

Besides, Rena knew all about his erectile problems. She had mitigated them. Erased them. With her and nobody else. Making her indispensable to his well-being.

But he had resisted, gone home. And now he and she were back together. Sort of.

He refused the offer of a giant martini. "How can you drink so much and stay on top of things?"

She gave him a lewd glance. He laughed, perfunctorily, not amused.

"Would you like to revisit that monastery?" she asked.

Leroy thought. What? It was now in enemy territory, part of a deal of land for peace.

"Of course, it's much changed. It's the center of a military think tank, guarded like nobody's business. The funny thing is that the same little monk is still there, absolutely unaware of the change. Think he'll remember us?"

"What the hell are you talking about? How could we get in there? And why?"

"To blow it to kingdom come," she said, sipping.

"Oh, no you don't. I've got a little but nice life over there. What I've lost I've compensated for. I volunteer in a humane shelter." He realized how ridiculous all this sounded to a committed patriot, ready to surrender her life for the cause. He thought he heard the rumble of the roller coaster, destroyed these many years, the taste of cotton candy, fudge, taffy that rolled and stretched between rollers. A kind of grown-up childhood. That was what Rena was for him. He turned teary eyes to her. "I can't. I won't. Do you understand? I love Israel, but this is too much."

She put her glass down, which made a tinkling noise as it touched a full glass the orderly had just set down beside it. They clearly wanted to make him drunk.

"Your little life," she said and paused. "It exists, doesn't it? Surrounded by a little sleep – I don't remember the exact words – as against many lifetimes, voluntary, chosen, as the chosen people are chosen, never to die, never to age, always able to down buckets-full of martinis, drink of the gods."

"Are you telling me you are one of the gods, that I am a plaything for you, that the explosion our intercourse causes is just one of a casual bunch of experiments, to see what the tiny people will do?"

"You've heard of 'turtles, turtles, all the way down'. Say I am one of the turtles just a few levels away from you, needing to put together scenarios in order to move up to turtles closer to the light."

Leroy brooded and then blurted, "And I am no more than a short series of steps. Nothing more. You don't care for me. I don't want to sound lugubrious, but I thought differently." All the while Leroy was thinking frantically of a way out. Hard to do in a chopper a mile away from land. Could he just jump out and hope that he would land back at home? Because Rena or her people could do such things. Risky, but no more than breaching the walls of a military complex.

"No," she replied as though he had spoken out loud, "you would merely smash yourself wherever you landed, Leroy, even in water. You know the math. By the way, there's something in that single martini you managed to consume that will take care of all your male problems forever, not only with me. That's the bonus. How? Do you live through the explosion?" She frowned. "Of that I'm not sure. I'm not privy to everything the upper brass does. Or if I'm as expendable as you. We'll just have to see. Take it as it comes."

Leroy was exasperated and let it show. "All part of a casual experiment. Rats in a maze. Man in amazement. I refuse. Take me home. Get out of my life. I thought you had. Now, do it for good." Leroy was quite heated. He checked himself and found that he was almost altogether in agreement with what he was saying.

The chopper made the usual sounds prior to landing. Leroy looked out the window at rising clouds of dust. He could see nothing. Gradually, as the sand settled, he made out a large metal door, dunes surrounding it. It was desert. How had the chopper traveled without stop between California and the Sinai desert? If it was really what it seemed.

"Here's your protective gear, false ID and the ability to speak Arabic, which you will find mouth-filling, I assure you." She laughed shortly. "There are quarters for the inhabitants. We will be designated checkers from central command."

Leroy thought furiously. I don't want to do this. It is immoral and wrong. He thought of something. Wait until they are all in there together, call out to guards, denounce Rena as a spy, get them to X-ray her and reveal the bomb, if it actually exists. He would be a hero and allowed to return home. To Belle. Who awaited. Her arms outstretched, birds cheerily calling.

Him.

## BOMBED

LEROY — CHAPTER 7

Let's assume, Leroy thought, that I am under constraints in some loony bin back home, drugged out of my mind, oblivious to the repressed tears of Belle, who has constantly stood by me, guided me, succored me, through my long and various and undistinguished lie. I mean, life. The brain is a various thing. Synapses can play tricks, lay traps, any number of non-events become real and immediate. I wasn't through with Rena, clearly, so my brain has resurrected her, out of whole cloth, to force me to go to the end of the line with her.

Which is? People have died of heart attacks during sleep, dreaming what is unsupportable. My diddling with sci-fi gives my brain the scenario and layout for its story. I can't change that. The nervous system is in place. Why not just enjoy it, so that I don't give myself that heart attack? Maybe I will wake up and lose the shackles, rejoining my joyous – albeit ageing – wife, finish off a respectable and respected nonagenarian?

"Are you through rationalizing, Leroy?" Rena gave him a frankly painful prod to the ribs, which didn't feel like a phantom poke.

"Did you decide on me before, during or after our first orgasmic encounter? I still am amazed that we did it under the pier, right in public if anybody had been around to witness it. And yet, it was the most satisfying bit of lovemaking I can remember."

"Leroy," Rena said, her eyes sparkling, "I have to admit that I share your distaste for public displays of the carnal. We really made love in a seedy hotel right off Hollywood Boulevard. I admit in your mind I changed the locale to a more romantic, daring place. We actually met at a lecture on the future of the Weitzman Institute of Advanced Mechanics. I was detailed to look for candidates for the institute. You asked the most intelligent questions. So I chose you. You were not very prepossessing – even mousy, with ill-fitting clothes, a dirty handkerchief, which you kept taking out and burrowing into your nose. Not very appealing, I can tell you."

Leroy blushed. Of course. It was all changed now that she had set the memory straight. But what of the under-the-pier caper?

"It all happened, but later. We won't go into it now, because we are approaching zero hour."

"I told you, I'll tell you again, I won't go through with it. Silly of me, but I want to continue my little life as long as possible. With Belle. Not with you. You are part and parcel of my past, Rena, and I don't want you in my life now. So, skedaddle."

"Such a funny term," Rena answered pleasantly. "Taken for future resonances. Now, let's go."

Downhearted, Leroy saw they were already half through the heavy iron door. Rena absently kicked a hummock of sand away, almost as though she had a shovel in her hands. Disregardful of the myriad of tiny earnest creatures making their homes inside it, a truth Leroy was more and more aware of, and he had to attribute this to his proximity to Rena. He had to give her that. At least that.

"Leroy," Rena whispered so as not to alarm the guards on either side of them, grim-faced men who could have been Arab or Israeli or beings from another planet mimicking humans, for god's sake! "I hope you're getting the point that you can alter reality by what you think about it. One of your sci-fi idols did it, remember? How do you think she got her ideas?"

"You mean I can exchange the bomb in your twat for extra ovaries, for example? Or make my sperm into something that won't interact with your fluids and so disable the bomb?" Leroy was really getting into this. He liked the idea of changing reality. It had been done for and to him for so long now he was really ready for a change.

"I didn't mean to imply it was all that easy. If you're being tested, experimented with, you'll have to figure out what's on the table, so to speak, what kind of a maze you are being put through. You have to find out whether you've been bred for generations for this sort of thing, like mice or fruit flies."

"And you, Rena? Are you part of the experiment or one of the experimenters?"

Rena squinted at him, and her face was beautiful, radiant even. He so wanted to go to her, kiss her passionately; he felt his body yearning toward her, as it had so many eons before. He made a motion.

She pulled back. "I didn't mean to turn you on, not so suddenly, so precipitously, as though you were falling down a steep cliff. I can't answer that. I don't have the answers. They are withheld from me. Not unlike for you. I suspect we will both be told before this is all over. What started in the market. No, no," and she put one of her lovely tapering aromatic fingers over his mouth, "don't bother asking me how I know about that. It's part of my DNA now. Like your shining pate. Not half unpleasant," she laughed, like little children laugh as they play, running her hand over his skull.

Leroy squirmed and shuddered pleasantly. It was somehow comforting that Rena did not entirely know what was happening and therefore did not control it. Which may mean that he could have a hand in deciding things.

He wondered what he looked like to the white-aproned men and women he was passing, who barely looked up as they went by. But it was as though their minds were open books to Leroy, growing coherent as he approached, strongly illuminated as they came next to one another, fainter as they passed. The separate things they knew and surmised grew into columns in Leroy's mind, not yet connected, but promising. As though there were a projected structure, with faint outlines, and the columns could become parts of the foundation. With growing excitement Leroy hastened his steps.

"Hold on, Buster, don't turn into Superman so fast. What you've got hold of is still just a dream. Keep that thought. But slow down."

Leroy could not remember being so happy before, so sure he was now in his element, he would turn the world around if given the chance. Did the scientists or technicians or whatever they passed know what happened to the contents of their brains? Were they part of the experiment or were they also being experimented on? How can you tell the dancer from the dance? Leroy recited to himself, part of a largely forgotten poem by an Irish writer.

Leroy thought happily, I am also the dancer and the dance.

## LEROY: DESIRE, FRUSTRATION, DREAD

LEROY — CHAPTER 8

That thought warmed him, as though he needed it. The temp was certainly in the mid-80s in here. He wondered if the creatures manipulating him were like lizards and needed heat to function. He wondered if they had leathery skins that were only temporarily transmuted into the softer hues of the human. Why not? Why should people from distant climes have to look like him? And why wouldn't they mimic his kind – to keep him from dying of fright, and not from some dire motive. His brain simply wasn't calibrated to deal with extra-terrestrials.

But, looking around at familiar physiognomies, he jeered at his childish need to turn everything into mystery. Rena also had no remote connection to extra-terrestrials. He frowned. Was he feeling guilty? He had strayed sexually before, more times than he could readily remember, so it wasn't that. And Belle had plenty to keep her occupied. No, not that. Creeping into his mind was a memory he had repressed.

Rena's pregnancy. Yes! There was that. It was why he left Israel in the first place. She had assured him she was protected. Then she informed him. The figures of her powerful father and mother began to close in, subtly but firmly, offering him wonderful advantages if he elected to stay, become husband and father, a scientist in the most respected of institutes of Israel, of the world, really.

Without portfolio. He knew about influence and the attitudes of the people around who obviously know that a position has been acquired through bribery or family. No thank you, was Leroy's response. But there was no pressure. Swallowing hard, Leroy remembered the bumpy bus trip to the doctor/abortionist. Rena flinched but held back the tears. She refused his hand. Helpless, Leroy watched the parade outside. Colorful Arabs, dour and somber Catholic priests, half-naked children, the constant din of horns, shouts, machinery, the smells of everything. He longed for quiet, for his ears, for his nose and tongue.

The office was a surprise. It could have been a synagogue, a place Leroy made sure not to visit. Except in this place was a desk and a severely dressed middle-aged woman with a rolodex. A record in paper!

"We have an appointment," Leroy mumbled, as Rena looked at the framed portraits on the walls of various famous rabbis of history and even before history, all with long impressive beards, some grim, others contemplative, some even giving forth with a slight smile. Rena appeared to be asking each of them a question, maybe the same question. Should I go through with this? Is it permissible? But Rena wasn't religious either, he thought, so he would ask her about this.

"Please make yourselves comfortable," the woman commanded, though the stiff chairs hardly gave any indication that was possible.

Rena continue to avoid Leroy's eyes. He examined himself. Could we cancel this? Just go with the flow? After all, what do I have waiting for me back home? At that moment he had not been able to remember that he did have a life in the States, a wife, a job, friends. That part of his brain was sidelined, as though for a motorcade of an important person. Some streets were not usable.

Did Rena know that, at the time? They were hurrying at such a pace, through room after room of people and exotic machinery that there wasn't time or space.

A man, indistinguishable from the dignitaries on the walls, hurried into the room, wrung Leroy's hand. It felt like he was commiserating for a death, which, of course, was the case. But why? Too many people on the planet anyway, an unwanted, uncalled for addition was hardly necessary. We should all be glad, Leroy thought, and then, guiltily; my blood line, my DNA, they're better than most.

I can't! he cried inwardly, as Rena was being led away by the doctor and an attendant. Nobody looked back. Leroy peered around for a magazine to distract him. At this distant time he couldn't remember whether or not he found one. It seemed ages, an attendant came out to announce: "It's over. The woman is fine. She will be able to reproduce at a later time at her will."

A distinctly strange speech, it seemed to Leroy. As though she would do it all by herself, asexually. Too much reading into a rote statement, Leroy dismissed the thought.

"Did you ever have another child? I mean, a child?" Leroy corrected himself hurriedly

"One was enough," Rena said neutrally. "But it's not what you think, what you remember. I have to tell you." She abruptly commandeered a couple of folding chairs, scraping them over the linoleum, leaving visible tracks. Leroy absently wondered if someone was going to be annoyed. So what?

"Haven't you ever wondered how he or she would come out? Grow up? Develop? Become?"

"Of course, who wouldn't? Look, I'm still sorry for what I put you through."

"Don't mention it," Rena said. "Did it ever occur to you as strange that a doctor's office would have all those rabbis hanging around?"

"Of course it did," Leroy said, "but it was Israel, people have strange bedfellows."

"Well, the doctor was also a rabbi, with very strong opinions about abortion. You know the Orthodox prohibit it altogether, even when the mother's life is in danger. Well, mine wasn't, as it happens. The baby's was. Remember the bomb? Oh, yes, it was in place even as far back as then. The doctor had to do some very fancy footwork to avoid it, avoid entangling, the umbilicus, all those things in there."

"Yes, yes," Leroy said.

"The long and short of it is: there was no abortion. There was a premature live birth. With my permission it was spirited away to a home the rabbi/doctor maintained for unwanted children. I visited from time to time."

"What's his name?" Leroy said, in shock.

"Moshe, Morris, to you, Moses to some, someone designated to part the Red Sea. I am the mother of a latter-day saint," she said, with a lilt and sob in her voice.

"You really believe that, don't you?" Leroy said, again attempting to take her hand, which she allowed, though limply. "Well, I can say I'm glad I have a son, so belatedly. Will I get to meet him?"

Rena smiled a little. "Oh, you will, you will. He's here, in this complex. In a way completely unknown to the Arabs, this laboratory invisibly fits inside one of their own, utterly self-contained. The bomb was never defused, merely replaced, not replaced, but re-placed. It now resides in Moshe, awaiting its time."

"You allowed a bomb to be emplaced in your own child?" Leroy said, appalled.

Rena shrugged. "Did I have a choice? When I woke up, the doctor told me, that's all. I never saw him again. I don't even know if he was produced for just that operation on me."

Leroy's head whirled. From the moment he was hailed in the market his life had been turned upside down. He didn't know what to believe. "Did your parents find out?"

Rena shook her head. "It had to be kept from them. They did meet him, but not as a grandchild, only as a *wunderkind,* who was able to recite chapter and verse of the most arcane texts. You know, on one of those old TV shows. Now we're getting close to the holy-of-holies. Watch your mouth."

Now Leroy was not so sure. Was he being

danced or was he dancing on his own, leading or following? Did it matter? Was this merely crazy things his brain was doing to his mind, and Belle was in the next room conferring with the hospice people, or was he really in the midst of a cosmic experiment, he of all the billions on the planet? Well, somebody has to win the lottery out of millions of tickets sold. Some agency has to win the residual prize of having sold the ticket. He wondered which of the two that was, Rena or Belle? If Belle was in on this, "this is your life, Leroy"?

What was fairly certain was that, in the here and now, he was about to meet the son he never knew he had.

## RENA OR BELLE

LEROY — CHAPTER 9

"OK," Rena said in an officious voice, "step inside this little cubicle, if you please."

She sounded like an old-fashioned attendant on an airplane, the kind wearing such a short skirt that when she bent over it was like a cartoon to see the goggle-eyed males on the plane follow her. But, Leroy thought, now wised-up to some extent, that was what he was supposed to think. Nonetheless, he obediently followed her into the room, which turned out to be kind of a replica of a police line-up. When his eyes adjusted to the dimness Leroy increasingly made out a line of females, all naked, standing straight-ahead, no expressions on their also-naked faces. And they were all known to Leroy!

He reeled, swerved to face Rena, but she wasn't there anymore. She was in the line-up of females standing behind glass, like so many mannequins in a store window. Somehow he knew it was the department store where he had been lost, sure he was never to be found, sure that his mother had deliberately lost him, hoping that some rich family would take him in, sad, but resigned that they could no longer support him.

But why? What had made him so expensive? His ailments? No, he was healthy enough, a few sniffles here and there, a little hernia, but ah! That undescended testicle, which kept having to be treated with an alloy of gold. Where were his parents to find such a thing? His father had had to learn to be a second-storey burglar, something against his strict Hebrew upbringing. It was a constant humiliation to don the mask, squeeze on the clinging shoes and check the rope for any loose strands. His mother would stand by the door, wringing her hands, tears falling like miniature waterfalls. Until his safe return, his pockets bulging with the raw materials for Leroy's next treatment. Dr. Strongin grew wealthy and powerful in the little town with the loot. Nobody thought to suspect him as go-between Leroy's father and the powerful underground, which bought weapons of mass destruction with the unholy takings.

Another item: Dr. Strongin had no scruples against experimenting with Leroy. What were his parents to do if Leroy turned into some sort of freak? They were nobodies. He could deny everything. And nothing about Leroy gave evidence anything was amiss.

Back in the present, Leroy frowned. Why was

he going over these unpleasant memories from the past? Look at the mannequins over there. They couldn't be alive, but why were they there anyway? For what purpose? And why was Rena among them?

Still, back to Dr. Strongin, whose memory, it appeared, seemed determined to play out. Rich, calm, as Leroy confronted him. Demanded to know why the treatments were continuing. His father was not getting any younger. Any night now he would be apprehended, perhaps shot, in any event consigned to prison. Leaving Leroy and his mother destitute, starving, and afraid. "Dr. Strongin, you've gleaned enough from my family to continue my treatments until their climax without further pay. I demand it."

"I can't do that, boy," Strongin murmured, smiling demurely.

Leroy saw with disgust the feminine, almost feline, motions of the doctor. He was also obese to the point of not being able to get up. He had a recliner that he could adjust to help him. Leroy moved swiftly. He crossed the room and yanked at the lever to raise and lower the doctor. He pulled it out of its joint. The doctor sprawled on the floor like a beached fish. Even his mouth opened and shut like a fish deprived of oxygenated water.

"You'll sign this declaration now," said Leroy

grimly with great resolution. He had had the forethought to bring the document. "Sign it. Or else."

Or else, what? thought the present Leroy. What did I have in mind? Kill him? The great whale of a medico. How? Nevertheless, he signed, to Leroy's great relief.

And admitted: "You're fine, boy. You don't need more treatments. In fact, the treatments were all bogus. But you have an advantage. All that gold has turned you into a kind of Croesus, as of old. Now everything you touch will have a gold effect."

"And what's that?" Leroy asked, horrified, worried that he was going to petrify.

"I don't know. The formula I used just came to me, out of the blue, and I followed it. I always follow my impulses," he said, unable to keep from boasting.

Leroy, disgusted, threw the lever at his feet. "Manage yourself, Doctor. You'll see no more of me." Saying this, he went to the restroom in the doctor's clinic and examined himself closely. Damn it, there they were, nicely descended, like little bells waiting to be rung.

Did his mother want to lose him? He would never know, because she had a seizure while searching for him and the next thing he knew he was in the hospital waiting for word.

Leroy with great force wrenched his mind back to the problem facing him at present.

A glow appeared on one of the walls. It gradually coalesced into a person, one with a phosphorescence so great Leroy had to shield his eyes.

"Sorry," the glow said, as a person, "it's hard to be less bright than nature and nurture intended. I am Morris, or Moshe, or Moses, as you choose, according to your belief system."

"I don't have beliefs. I am a scientist, damn it. Everybody around here insists on forgetting that, including me. And why do you glow like that?"

The person who appeared once the glow had dimmed, Leroy noted, had severely regular features and a head of ropy blonde hair, which he tossed as he spoke, like a teen-aged girl in the San Fernando Valley, shrugged. "The gold. It's the gold."

Leroy stared. So that was why the Strongin episodes came back to him so strongly. From Leroy to this person, this Moshe. His son. Leroy's eyes misted over. "I am so sorry we tried to get rid of you, son, I really am, but I just had to get used to the idea. Of being a father."

Moshe shrugged. "Do you want a hug?"

This question seemed so banal Leroy had to laugh, which broke the tension. "Not particularly. But you could explain the line-up of naked females surrounding us, all of whom I have had relations with, some quite questionable. Also, your mother is in there and I think it's particularly inappropriate for you to view her naked body. I mean, regardless of where I am, on earth or some other place, there are customs and mores that need to be followed."

Just then all the mannequins relaxed, some standing on one foot, some turning in place, some lighting a cigarette, but all looking out at Leroy, who blanched, struck by the simultaneity and intensity of their gazes. "What do I do about them?" Leroy gasped.

Moshe laughed, quite at his ease. "They are all the gold standard, but you must make your peace with them. You left them all hanging, one way or another, with one excuse or another. You see, Belle is there too. Didn't you recognize her?"

Leroy stared. Belle was there, with her favorite parrot on her shoulder, and the damned parrot was also staring at him, even more accusingly than the others.

# NOTHING VENTURED

## LEROY — CHAPTER 10

Leroy had to sit down. Actually, his legs wilted from under him. A chair appeared. He felt the gentle hands of his son press on his shoulders from behind. It was not a hostile pressure. In fact, the whole atmosphere was one of discovery rather than accusation. But surely he had wronged every one of the mannequins at one time or another. It was true. He had promised each and every one of them his hand in the future. He could see the hand, and an arm behind it reaching from now to then and, then, one after another of the mannequins turned and set out confidently toward the body, sure of his concern and even love, though none of them was so naïve as to think that now was forever. They knew he was married, but they still felt they had a greater hold on Leroy, even a greater right.

Moshe's increasing pressure seemed to say that the mannequins were not entirely in the right. Nay, that they might be even more to blame than Leroy, who had not sought them out, he remembered. In fact, it took more than one invitation before he succumbed to the tinkle of the golden testicles swinging and tingling inside his pants.

His son, he and the testicles were related. They were intimately joined, forever, it seemed. Whatever is animating this fantasy – for it was thus Leroy was justifying the whole thing – obviously held great store on the magic metal, which of course is the metal that motivates most human endeavor, most human literature, all of human art and architecture, the basis for all currency, even pounded to airy thinness (à la John Donne), the magic substance that prevents fogging of outer space vehicles.

"Moshe, you are made of gold," Leroy said, turning, while regretting this necessitated the removal of his son's magic hands, "but you are animated, you are alive, you are not like Croesus' daughter, who he turned into solid gold, to his eternal grief and loss."

Moshe laughed easily. "What you have here in these women, Daddy, is not punishment in the usual sense. You are only being brought back to an earlier era, one that may have actually transpired, or may not have, so that you may react to each of them. Notice that you have seen them as different women, although they all wear the same expressionless face. In fact, notice carefully, there is not really a face at all."

Leroy turned, his residual hair standing on end, and saw what Moshe said was veritably true. There was a kind of swarming where a face ought to be. So many faces were there moving and interchanging so rapidly as to be a blur, a swarm. But how? He distinctly remembered each affair. Each delicious recounting of old stories which were no more than a bore to his wife, new to the "conquest." Except it was he who was conquered, losing some of his standing in eternity each time it happened. If in fact he was in some place that could be called "eternity."

Could it be that he was as anonymous a swarm as these females? Not chosen from the teeming billions on the planet but actually *created* as an amalgam and fitted, like a tooth into the jawbone of his species.

"Don't ponder that, Papa, you are as real as I am, standing here, you sitting there. If you like, we are both experimental, test tube creatures of a greater power that wants only to understand. Perhaps, having created us and sent us on our way, they went out for a drink or a movie and only later went back to the lab to see what developments had developed. I'm not saying this is so, but if it makes you happier – "

"What do you expect of me? I don't quite believe in your humility, Moshe."

Moshe or Morris or Moses shrugged. "Well, then, let's get to the test. You are desired to approach each of the women, in turn, and say and do what occurs to you at the moment. In a moment of giddiness, which will pass, you will return to the moment of truth."

"Is that like when the bullfighter stabs the bull, that kind of moment of truth?"

M or M or M laughed. "You compare yourself to a killer. I never did that. Perhaps you killed some hopes in these women, young usually, much younger than you. How do you know there wasn't in the back of her mind the fact that you had a fat pension awaiting you on retirement? In one aboriginal tribe men always marry much younger women. They die and their widows take up with much younger men. Everybody dies happy."

"Not my tribe," Leroy said gloomily. "Far from it."

M gestured with his finely tuned chin.

"OK, I'm on it," Leroy said, with resignation.

The first one already had suffered an early abortion. Not Leroy's offspring. Leroy was young, so young he didn't have a notion of the yawning trap laid for him, an adolescent pining to leave his family's lair. Now as Leroy approached, her arms preternaturally reached out to him, it even seemed more than two of them, as his shoulders were encircled and also his genitals. Ecstatically, he fell into her body as into a great yellow pudding, as she was blonde – probably even from birth. Some years went by, her dissembling caused a basic reordering of parts and she gradually went bananas (also yellow), while Leroy frantically searched for someone with a cure. As he held her trembling frame one night, she shook herself into pieces and was thereafter never again seen. Nobody inquired after her, to Leroy's surprise, as he expected to be arrested for her disappearance. Apparently, even every record of her disappeared along with her atoms.

Leroy felt himself being pushed back into the waiting chair.

"That wasn't so bad," observed Moshe, "maybe the next one will be a little more traumatic, so gird yourself, Pappy of mine."

Leroy looked on the next one, who turned shabby and gaunt as he peered at her. Was he responsible for this turnabout? He rose, with difficulty, as his joints didn't seem to be working very well. He limped toward her. As he did, she staggered, a bottle fell from her nerveless hand and shattered on the sidewalk. She refused his helping hand. He looked into her face, visible now, at her gaping mouth, innocent of many teeth, and he was aware of an awful stench.

He knew the smell of rotting vegetables. Also flesh. This was flesh.

## ROTTING FLESH

LEROY — CHAPTER 11

It wasn't so much her rotting flesh, he was made aware of the awfulness of the entire world, as though he had just been fitted with the nostrils of a dog multiplied countless times. He smelled the cold sweat of a caveman holding shut the mouth of his mewling infant against the sniffing, prodding of a cave bear eager to tear all of them into little pieces, in order to feed his own cub. He smelled the armpits of a swordsman in an arena whose ears rang with the shouts and jeers of the spectators, avid for blood, it didn't matter which, the rampant steer's, or his, or a rival swordsman's. The smell of freshly spilled guts. The open latrines in a medieval street, flies thick on the feces of humans and horses, pigs and sheep, indiscriminately mixed. He was even able to sense the pheromones of insects desperate to attract a mate before their so-limited moments were spent.

No human before him was privy to such a plethora of odors. Why him?

"Daddy, fear not, everything comes to an end, or a pause, and this also."

"Why me? Wasn't it an accidental meeting in the market? Or was there something about me that attracted your people? I am so ordinary," Leroy said, honestly for a change. "The world has always been a cesspool, renewing itself with plants and flowers, but people! The people are too awful. Look, you have my permission to get rid of them. Your people clearly don't stink."

M laughed easily, not embarrassed. "Elimination is a certainty, Daddy." He glanced at the swerving and weaving scarecrow of a figure of a woman standing a few feet away. "Shall we re-commence?"

Leroy thought, do I have a choice? He held himself erect. He hesitated, then held out his hand. The woman wobbled toward him and snatched it, took it to her mouth, to her lips and slobbered over it, making the motions of a kiss.

Repelled, yet fascinated, Leroy searched his memory for any sliver of this woman, this former woman, now only a smelly walking corpse.

"I'm Eugenia, Eugenia, don't you remember me?"

As she spoke she regained some figment of her former self. A student, from Lithuania, an orphan of WWII, he immediately loved her wavy red hair that caught every fugitive sun beam that managed to find its way in through the always-filthy windows of the evening school he labored in. The only job he could find while searching for a doctor who could cure his child wife.

She remained after class to ask him a rhetorical question. No, it wasn't that. It had to do with correcting a letter of appeal for aid from the war orphans board. From where? From Lithuania? Was there such a thing? Was it trumped up? Did she smell on him the desperation for nearness and touch? She could offer it. Free of charge. For now. Like the first five pounds of weight street scales used to offer, but you had to insert a nickel to get the rest. She was like that. First touch free, maybe even the first intercourse, but then –

He was glad to correct the letter. She stood close. Strands of her silken hair quivered on his cheek. She apologized prettily and stood a little further off. But the damage was done. Leroy was hooked, he was swooning.

In no time they were in a coffee shop. Also in no time further, she suggested a darkly lit bar. Leroy ordered beer, but she murmured whisky. Leroy calculated how much time he had before his wife would wonder. So, not this time. But they touched. He drove her home. He was able to ignore the smell of whisky on her breath.

"You may kiss me, if you wish. I am so grateful," she simpered in her delicious EasternEuropean accent, redolent of culture and mystery.

Leroy gladly did it, shocked when her vivacious tongue slivered into his mouth and explored the inner sides of his teeth. Actually, he didn't much like it, as an earlier girlfriend had nearly blocked his windpipe doing the same thing. But this girl's tongue was especially brisk and business-like. She withdrew before he could gasp. She took his head in both hands and pressed it to her exuberant bosom.

Well, Leroy was hooked. But before long, he realized how expensive whisky could be, in numbers. Even if she was so ready to fall into the nearest bed afterwards, pretending total willingness, passively drunk, easily made naked.

How to get out of this, Leroy wondered, surfeited with her, a little put off by her hygiene. That is, lack of it. After the first few bouts, Leroy wondered if he could suggest a shower, perhaps *à deux,* before coitus. She didn't feel the need even afterward, though of course Leroy had to wash off the evidence of their encounters.

Leroy quit the job. She didn't know where he lived. Maybe she would forget. Forget about him. He prayed.

But he saw her again. On the street. She was begging. In rags. Her hair all snarled. Leroy was horrified. Had he been responsible for this? What should he do? He couldn't take her in. He already had one nut case on his hands. He decided to hurry away. Did he feel her eyes digging into his back?

"No," said the ever-cheery Moses, "she didn't see you. With those bleary eyes I imagine she could see very little. It wasn't long before a brute took her into a back alley, had his nasty way with her and left her for dead. What you see here is a reproduction of her last days."

"But why?" Leroy pleaded, totally disgusted with himself. "I could have called someone, anyone, to help."

"No," Moses said thoughtfully, "it wasn't supposed to happen. All the information was in. You were needed elsewhere. In another situation."

The figure of the scarecrow was back in the lineup, quite still, emanating no odor, nothing of the living person.

## SHATTERED CHILDHOOD

LEROY — CHAPTER 12

Morris said, slowly, ponderously, "It might have been so traumatizing for you to have to be attached to a woman whose actions you could never predict. Children like to be able to know what is going to happen next. I know I felt that way."

Leroy saw a chance to peer into the previous life of a life he never knew existed, not before this moment. "What was it like to never know your father?"

"Not so big a deal as you might think. Rena kind of disowned her parents, who never approved of my existence. In fact, they tried to ignore it. So I felt a little like a cloud, heavy today, dissipated tomorrow, never substantial. That's why my place here with you gives me more weight even as we speak. More reality, so to speak. A kind of warmth emanating from I know not where."

"Allow me not to believe you," Leroy said, without anger.

M shrugged. "Can you go with the possibility that I am as much in the dark as you are about where you are and why?"

"Given that a whole passel of fairly naked females prominent in my past, are all standing still here, and so are you, and Rena too, somewhere in the backstage, yes, I find it pretty unreal."

M continued as though he hadn't heard. "It wasn't long into my life that I started to know I was a walking bomb, taking over for my mother, who just wasn't as mobile as I was. I was trained to infiltrate. I can become like almost anybody at any time. How I am for you is like that. Actually, what do I seem to be to you?"

Leroy thought. "Ideal. You seem ideal. If I had a son he would look like you. I think."

M nodded happily. "That's good. I'm glad you approve. It means that I have succeeded at least in that. I can hope for more. Anyway, I haven't had to blow myself up, as yet, as nothing has been important enough. Not until now."

"Until now?"

"The experiment may be reaching its conclusion. A foot may be descending to squash the entire termite mound, so to speak. That is, the world."

Morris didn't seem particularly perturbed by his news, if it was news.

"Moses, if your namesake means anything, you are a kind of savior to your people. If in fact they have descended or ascended to be one of us, doesn't that mean you can be a voice for us? Advocate for us? Delay the final hour? Stop it?"

"Do you want me to? Your life doesn't seem to carry much weight, Daddy. You have played fast and loose with a number of your species."

The atmosphere of this little room seemed closer and closer, as though oxygen were being withdrawn. Leroy's mind began playing him tricks, and he found himself in another place and time again. A different woman, no less ghastly than those others: his mother and he were walking together on a crowded sidewalk, like in NYC, her gnarled palm outstretched. In Leroy's hand was a tattered hat in which were already a few rumpled dollar bills. He was hoping that they would buy him some bread and milk rather than another bottle of rotgut for his mother. He wondered if he was doomed to the same sort of anchoring to the bottle. As he grew older, still attached to the hag, he was at the same time her child and the occasioner of her downfall, at least a good part of it, because he could remember his association with her at the night school. How can that be?

His brooding was cut short by a sharp slap to his cheek. Burning, he turned to the woman who administered it. "Pay attention! The nice man is speaking to you."

Leroy, with burning cheeks, turned to the man, and without too much surprise, recognized him as himself in a later incarnation. Somehow, he realized there were just so many iterations available to the creatures that were manipulating him.

How different is this from the thousand images available to the smallest humblest fly?

"How about I take you away from all of this, little boy, clean you up and take you to the grandparents who will be glad, after all, to take you in, given that your mother is inadequate?"

The little boy was torn. The grotesque scarecrow was all he knew. Leroy was, had been, in the market, possessed of his knowledge of where he was, and that was all. How else? If he took the hand of the stranger, now, it meant believing in a different future. Part of a cosmic experiment, of which this might be the final brick in the wall, after which – ?

So, Leroy didn't want to make a movement. He stood stock-still.

Moshe's voice broke the silence, and the New York street dissolved back into the dark room, women lined up before him. Gently, he said, "The outcome doesn't depend on one action, Leroy. Consult your golden testicles, which you bequeathed to me, thankfully. Let them ring." He made a self-consciously silly gesture of tinkling, then laughed. "I'm growing fond of my daddy. I hope we both live. Thrive. Rena is so serious.

I'm hoping for some fun." He looked toward the still-standing figures.

Leroy hoped he himself was not about to disport himself with any of them, with his son attending.

## TINNITUS

LEROY — CHAPTER 13

Moshe's outlines blurred. He looked annoyed. "I don't always agree with my mother," he explained, distracted, while he seemed to Leroy to be not only blurring, but vibrating at a terrific rate. His molecules appeared to be jarring, at war with each other. As though he were a being composed of many galaxies, each galaxy composed of trillions of stars, and within each star multitudes of planets, the inhabitants of which were engaged in stupendous debate about something so tremendous no one entity was able to describe it all. And so everything went ballistic.

Then gone. Moshe, Moses, Morris. Gone. His son. Gone before Leroy had gotten any chance to know him. At all. A cruel thing, Leroy thought, as loudly as he could.

Rena stood there. Smiled. "You didn't want him to begin with. How do you think you can make up all those years struggling and straining in an orthodox society to raise a bastard? My own parents didn't want to speak to me. I became a living, walking bomb because I wanted to leave something for him, a legacy he could be proud of. I would watch him from another world. Oh, I know that's nonsense, superstition. What if I am an animated puppet for the purposes of entities so far advanced to me that I cannot even imagine their motives."

"You mean, none of this is real?" quavered Leroy.

"Real enough," Rena said wearily. "What do you hear?"

Leroy had more questions, but he was beginning to hear something: apparently another test was in progress. He imagined white-coated giants waving pencils of light and indecipherable symbols appearing on something like clouds. The tinnitus which had bothered him for many years was suddenly much louder and higher in pitch and continued to go louder and higher. Leroy was aware that if this process was to go on much longer his ears would burst, blood would gush and he would fall dead.

In which empyrean? Not to worry about that. His life was in the balance.

Now the tinnitus began to segregate sounds, like an improbably vast orchestra composed of instruments not found on Leroy's planet. He was given the power to hear the music of things, as the alien entities could. He heard and saw trees and flowers and dirt and clouds, masses of people congregated, earth-moving machines, fleets of all kinds of aircraft, tunnel-digging mole-like creations, all with their singular tone, each vibrating at a rate even greater than that which had annihilated Morris, Moses, Moshe.

If it had, and had not merely translated him into another form of matter, as the entities seemed able to do without stint.

Leroy held his breath, because the symphony was so unutterably beautiful. As a pedagogue he wanted to be able to express it to a dull class, hoping to raise its communal level to something attentive, focused, rapt.

Yes, he wanted rapt, he wanted rapture, he realized how deficient in that quality his whole life had been. He realized that when one of the ladies in the market was squeezing a fruit or a vegetable, she was distilling its particular music that came only to her ears, because Leroy's were far too thick and dull to hear.

But were they somehow promising him a place at the table if he fulfilled certain obligations? What? Leroy wanted to jump up and down, he so wanted to be chosen. But how?

The undifferentiated sound of the tinnitus was really music, if he had the wit to hear. "Now I am wised-up," Leroy said out loud, very earnestly.

Rena walked around and kicked a piece of cloud. She seemed distracted. She didn't appear to be very interested in the goings-on. The piece of cloud reacted with disdain, emitting a series of sounds like an angry arpeggio on a piano and a drum. But even this was music to Leroy's ears. Every sound included every other sound, a whole catalogue of world music from the beginning of creatures pounding on hollow logs to cricket-like creatures rubbing their legs together to attract a bug of the opposite sex.

Leroy imagined gossamer wings to his body. While at it, why not imagine two sets, like dragonflies have? So be it. He thrummed them together, delighted at the complex sounds that were produced. Now to fly, Leroy thought, why not?

High up, clouds below, his ears now able to differentiate endless combinations of sounds making up cantatas, symphonies, rhapsodies, etc. never heard on earth, and which, Leroy thought, if he could reproduce, would make his fortune and his name forever.

Then, into his plethora of sound, came the question: "Why would you want to be known after you die? Because you will die. Perhaps you will die of the heart-bursting beauty of what you produce, whether it be music, or literature or machinery."

"Like Rena," Leroy gasped, "I don't care if the work is so incendiary it kills me. To have the feeling, the expression, the ecstasy of it. That's enough." He thought of his pedestrian life with Belle. How he could have thrilled her with his compositions.

The voice came into the center of his ears. "Remember, Leroy, you don't play any instrument. Not the piano, even. You can't express any of this. You are too deficient."

Leroy hunkered down. He said, shrewdly, "You folk can have me do whatever is your will. If you want to give my species something wonderful, like Shakespeare, Mozart, Bach, you can. You probably did this already with those world-shakers. When did you appear to Einstein, Faraday, Newton? Huh? I feel I have the right to an answer. You've played with me a lifetime's worth already."

Rena pushed the clouds away, releasing a veritable world of playing drums and shrilling oboes. "All right, Leroy, come with me. Into another part of the monastery."

# DIVERTICULOSIS

## LEROY — CHAPTER 14

The passageways through which Rena led Leroy had waxy walls, thread-like hairs that quivered as though responding to their motion, as though sentient. Leroy had no trouble believing they actually were, after sensing the trees, leaves, bugs, just about everything in creation having an interior-dwelling intelligence.

Maybe he was being educated for some purpose? Having been selected randomly, he was now being coached in an intensive way. In any event, to his relief he was no longer facing the disquieting array of mannequins. Despite their facelessness he knew absolutely which woman in his past each was. Only Rena had a face and an accusing set of speeches. As though she was unwilling to be his guide but had no choice, no free will.

Free will! At this point he knew such a concept was utterly meaningless. When had he last trod this way or that before deciding? Epigenetically, meaning, after all of his genes were in order, knowing where they belong, what they need to do, whether now or much later. Sleeping now, gathering strength and volition, rushing with all their considerable might to the barrier, crashing it down, yelping in joy when they overcome the passivity before adolescence or senescence, overcoming any barrier with the same inane vigor.

Leroy was in the position of finding his parts ludicrous, laughable, but so strong as to prevent him from any sort of intelligence.

Rena, it felt to him, was guiding this self-mockery with altogether too much grim satisfaction. All right, she had a primary right. She had produced a child, but never had any joy of him, as he was now back in some part of this weird place, no longer having anything to do with him or with his mother.

"Do you get to spend time with Moshe, etc.?" he asked, very tentative, as he didn't want to provoke an outburst.

Rena kept plowing ahead, not bothering to answer, though her stiff shoulders told enough of a tale.

Leroy had the odd feeling that he was climbing his own skeleton, the further he penetrated into the catacombs of this place. In fact, in niches in the walls, small skeletons began to appear, giving way to larger and larger, more aggressively placed or modeled, as though to frighten the passerby, the onlooker, to remind him or her of the ultimate end of things.

"I suppose you are owed some explanation of this," Rena said, in a resigned tone of voice. "There is some sort of reward suggested for me, like a carrot on a stick, and I am a furry rabbit sort of creature. Anything is possible," she said.

Leroy tried to look sympathetic, though in fact he was scared and tired. As soon as he thought this he was no longer scared and tired. But immediately, he was suspicious of this sudden change. How he was manipulated. Like a rag doll. Or like Rena, a rabbit. He had to giggle. Rena as a rabbit! And she so formidable! At this sound she turned and glared at him. Softened. Said, "I should thank you for getting on that plane at all, I suppose, having been put away for so long. But where?" she asked herself, not really speaking to Leroy, "I'll never know, unless one of the entities bothers to step up to the microphone."

Instantly, as though summoned, jagged thoughts cropped up. Leroy had to mentally walk carefully not to be impaled by one of them. What would happen then? Leroy was not about to find out.

He was walking inside his own intestines.

Forget how that is possible. Maybe it is always true, Leroy reasoned. He remembered the fact that 9/10 of what is inside our bodies is not human tissue but foreign matter, all living, either harmoniously in health or at war with an adjoining colony. Now, Leroy had the vision to see that within each weathered hole in his colon existed a universe, maybe several, discontinuous with that or those in another fissure. Blood pooled dangerously behind each hole, held back by a thin wall of tissue. As though the universe were in dire danger all the time if pressure increased. Did the denizens within know about their danger? Or about the others, Leroy was big enough to see several of?

Must be. Someone was noticing. Because Leroy had been brought here. For some reason. Rena too. She didn't seem surprised. Maybe she has been brought here before. She surely wasn't here on her own initiative. She was through with him eons ago! Before Belle. Before Belle? Chronology no longer was part of his makeup. Leroy shook his head as though to clear it, pointless movement.

"It's the multiverse you've read about," Rena said, tonelessly, a tour guide bored with her passengers. "Each lesion in the colon is a universe with its own rules. It is not possible to traverse the distance between them, and they all obey different rules of physics and mathematics."

"Which one is controlling us?" Leroy asked, shrewdly, he thought.

Rena shrugged. "How should I know? For all I know there is a superior intelligence that moves, that motivates them all. That has put them into your body, that gives you the knowledge that you're walking inside your own body, all these universes living there."

"Is this true of everybody, everybody's body?"

"It may be. I don't want to think of the vastness, the microscopic smallness, the motivation, the powers."

"Rena, was this all in the making when we bedded down in the monastery in the desert a lifetime ago?"

"It probably had already happened to us inside one of these worlds, Leroy." Rena seemed on the verge of tears. Leroy knew she was frustrated that she wasn't in control of her own destiny. Even the word sounded its own mockery. "We are going to descend into one of them. How, I don't know. The passage is likely to be sickening, or will knock us out. Or I may disappear, just like the others. Did you have a special feeling for me?" she asked suddenly, to Leroy's surprise, showing a vulnerability he hadn't thought possible for her.

"Of course I did," Leroy hurriedly answered, wondering if she had a special insight into his motivations. Had he felt something for her? Was it more than the physical need a male homo sapiens had for the female of the species? And his lies? If they were lies? He nodded, "Yes, I have it still,

Rena," and made to take her hand in his but the solid flesh became ropy and soapy as he touched it. His eyes filmed over. Milky. Everything milky. Before his sight totally rejected him, he thought he saw a tower of blood surging behind one of the pocks, ready to overwhelm everything in its way.

## SPHINCTER

### LEROY — CHAPTER 15

I want to know, to have, a purpose! Leroy cried silently.

I want to know where all this is heading. There has to be a reason, more than bumping into two mysterious women in a market, influences affecting me and all that surrounds me, bringing in everybody I have ever contacted. How can there be such an intelligence that coordinates such a panoply of inputs. A being whose switchboard complexity lights up everything in a sensible pattern?

All the while he felt he was descending and ascending in a whirlpool that was simultaneously accreting and stripping him of everything he knew. All he was. He was being outfitted for a new purpose. As though millennia of evolution were being stripped away and a new set of years fitted onto his sturdy frame. As though the human skeleton were able to accommodate numerous possibilities. Yes, that is possible, Leroy judged, trying to maintain a certain equilibrium in his mind, cradled inside a skull that was changing with speed inconceivable.

Rena stood by and watched. She had seen all

this before, apparently. When had she been chosen? Before she met him, Leroy? And was she the reason he was now undergoing this both cosmetic and basic change? Maybe he was peripheral to her, rather than the other way around. That would be a modest comfort. Finished with her, Leroy would vanish or be set back, like a chessman, on his tiny board. Forgetting everything. Possible that the simple folk around him had been manipulated at some time, just like him, and been ordered to forget, delete the whole affair.

How many others have traversed their own skeleton and peered into their diverticuli? Is this humor on the part of some thing or being?

Questions. No answers. No one was even listening. He thought he saw the corridor, somehow. He was both in and not in it. He was remembering it. Had he ever seen a picture of his colon's pockmarks? He visualized a genial doctor informing him that most middle-aged people have them. His were bleeding. Why? The doctor shrugged. Nobody knows why, he said, absently, clearly thinking about his next patient, maybe one with pendulous breasts, the kind doctor favored, with a tang and flavor he could manipulate. Doctors are human, too, aren't they? Leroy pleaded. He was sorry he had seen a picture of the little ruts. Naturally, he saw nothing living inside them. Who would? The doctor, if he knew, would be in line for a huge prize. Colonies inside the colon! might read the headline. Can we contact them? Do they understand language? Hooray. Extra-terrestrials found inside us! Scientists feverishly strive for microphones small enough, sensitive enough!

Ridiculous! The whole thing, ridiculous. Leroy was undergoing a kind of special psychosis, compounded of fatigue of his brain and hysteria of his boredom. It was Belle's fault, with her dreary preoccupation with the avian creatures. Well, did she want to fly away, from him? Wasn't that at the heart of it? Her so-deep desire, added to his intense boredom with his life and guilt for former life. That could have animated his colonies of diverticuli to a kind of need to make contact. But without giving away secrets they hoarded to themselves.

One of the pocks? A consortium of them? No, they were separate; Rena would not have misinformed him. They did not have the ability to communicate with one another. Perhaps. Perhaps. He was enlisted to make the contact among them. He was a kind of wormhole personified by way of which or whom the separate galaxies could contact and even become more powerful, maybe totally able to regulate and control every body.

No, maybe his one body was enough for them

all, living inexpressible distances from one another as they are, even if millimeters from one another in the world Leroy inhabited.

With all this activity why hadn't he been made aware of it before now? Well, maturity counts for something. Not every body counted diverticuli among its deficits. That is, deficits as seen by the good doctor. His diagnosis and suggestion? Let him operate to cut out the offending sector of colon. Reattach the parts free of holes and with a hope they might not recur. Gone forever. Losing only a mere fraction of colon. How much? To what result? Oh, maybe a touch of diarrhea, of bloat, of gas. Because the colon really, really likes its great length, the way a snake would not be happy at half its length. The better to digest the odd calf or deer, you know.

Leroy was made to think: what will they do with the excised part? Throw it away? Burn it? His mind reeled at the enormity of it. Whole galaxies incinerated, with the incredible accretion of experience and knowledge. As though it had never existed.

Only his colon? Only? It is not possible to put all their eggs in one basket, so to speak. I must be one of multitudes. Some greater intelligence is manipulating all this. And making this knowledge available to me, now, right now.

Leroy turned blindly to Rena, who seemed to have assumed human shape and consistency again. "Am I ancillary to you or are you only an addition to me?"

For the first time, Rena looked at him the way she used to in the dingy rooms they rented, when their affair was new, or nearly so. "Why not just let it happen? The way you swung yourself over the berm and faced a plethora of Arabs, with your untested weapon, that turned out, in the battle, to be so effective? You were brave! You were so unconcerned for your safety. What was important was the idea, the concept. For it you would have gladly died. I know it. I was so proud. I didn't mind, in fact, I was so proud, to be bearing your seed."

Leroy looked at her with great commiseration. "And then I forced you to terminate it. What a cad!"

"You were torn, Leroy. Much like the way you are now. You want to help the tinies to their great consummation, which will perhaps terminate our species in the process, or even amalgamate it, bring it to a perfection inconceivable to limited intelligences like ours."

Leroy was being hurried at terrific speed toward the end of the looping tube that is the colon in all its giant and small parts, with all the various organs and chemicals working on it to extract the living stuff that makes up the body, while leaving the great river of indigestibles to break upon the sphincter, a great dam blocking exit to the world outside.

"What am I thinking?" Leroy wondered. "Rhapsodizing on waste that will end up in that receiver of all waste, the lowly toilet. This is loathsome. And not to mention, silly."

Feeling himself riding and roiling on said waste, Leroy could see countless items being borne along with him. People, houses, tall buildings, great fields with migrating animals, cemeteries. All carried along in a great flood, all the accoutrements of his people.

Against the adamant sphincter, refusing to give way before its time.

## IT'S TIME

LEROY — CHAPTER 16

A great noise of flapping recalled to Leroy his other life. The one in which Belle played such a large role that he might have hidden entirely within her voluminous garments. Under her arms swerved and voluted a whole life of life. Leroy strained his tinnitus-afflicted ears to try to make sense of the discrete noises. Scientists had tried to decipher what they called singing of great whales. The differentiated barking of seals carries perhaps a subtle message to other seals. Even our language, that of humans, sometimes makes sense, Leroy thought, wittily, he thought, and then with savage contempt – what am I doing piddling with linguistics at a time like this?

Again, time. He was with Rena in the desert. He was with Belle in the aviary. In the market with agents of the Unknown. Or simply common friendly women. The light surrounding the outside beggar went out. Winked out. As though his existence had lighted some aspect of this game and was no longer relevant – thus extinguished. A living being, snuffed so casually, cannot mean much to who or whatever is doing this to me, Leroy thought.

The lack of a ruler or measuring stick of any kind was a frustration. Leroy imagined himself in a dinghy, narrow but of infinite length, which, if he could but walk its length might explain some of the phenomena he had suffered. Like a space ladder. He imagined himself climbing it, through changes of weather, atmosphere and lack of it, the creatures he might encounter on his way, both real and hallucinatory.

Wasn't this whole thing an illusion? Get over it, he told himself sternly. Its time has come, a voice inside the tinnitus started to say, or rather, had been saying for some time, but only comprehensible now, right now, the now that is right, the now that is always right, because there is no other now than the now that is now-ing.

Leroy shook his head as though to dislodge an annoying beetle or fly. And the denizens might actually be in his hair. What foolishness! he thought. I don't have any hair. Silly, he thought, the pits where hair used to grow are there, if you know how to look for them. If you are small enough to fit inside one. A cradle for another kind of critter.

If I am floating and tumbling inside the cloaca of a contemporary human being, he thought, then there must be a multitude of experimental animals in process, an infinite number. Was that comforting, to be one of a featureless horde? Not singled out for express punishment for what he did in life, not his choice anyway, since all this definitely precluded anything like freedom of will. Even going to a market for orange juice. Giving or not giving a dollar to the usual beggar in front, whose full face he remembered, he had never seen. Did that mean the beggar might not have a face? That the unnamed other hadn't bothered fashioning one for him? Or if Leroy had given him more money would that have changed history?

Or is a deity something with a warped sense of humor, shoehorning himself/itself into a beggar-like figment? With fly-like eyes to be able to peruse an entire landscape at a glance. Did it exist outside of time, in a forever place? Has it laid down a scent-trail for mythologists to follow with their eager nostrils aflare?

Does it bore easily, so that it sets populations afire with conflicting ambitions, just to see what they will do? But it already knows in advance what they will do, doesn't it? Every conclusion is already in its premise, both in the molecular world and in the macro world. But those terms become porous, even liquid, with no defining borders when you posit an intelligence on both sides of an issue, the before and the after.

When such a creature decides to mate, do worlds shake? Does the other sex, or whatever, take on god-like qualities, and can it sometimes decide to rebel?

Female creatures on earth do. Leroy ached to be able to lay hands on Belle's shoulders, where the wings fit, when they are appropriate. But the entity had decided to make Rena primary outlet to the world. Ignoring Belle. Or did he have to struggle through something to get back to her, to his own place in the made-up continuum, for that was what Leroy was forced to conclude. The world is real only so far as we can imagine it.

One thing remained clear. Destruction was in the air. That was his sense of it. Its time. Not his time. Its time. Maybe arbitrarily made up, but it was there. He had moved through it, back through it. Something was required. A kind of chess game. He played, he was played. Is there a difference? Clear difference?

A decision. Shall Rena go through with the abortion or not? Easy to say now, when the fetus was all grown up and beautiful, full of energy and life, expectancy, verve. All the things he, Leroy, lacked.

Noah's ark suggested itself, tentatively. Even shyly. Two by two, all creation boarded, expectant, looking forward to the new grazing, savannah, forest, plain.

Or dumbly, obedient.

Does Leroy obey the summons to disobey?

Does the entity deal only with paradox, as the only formulation shared by it and humans? A long thin, delicate, lacy strand, smelling of vanilla. Vanilla?

Sure, the neutral flavor, not giving away its origins or its destinations.

Dog with open smiling jaws asking for the ball to be thrown. A pointless exercise. The only kind.

Never again to have a female asking the unanswerable question: do you love me? Truly? Not only lust? Will you be in love with me when I start to look like Belle or Rena? Wrinkles hide the rutted tracks of aquifers on the distant planet.

Will you take the bomb? asks a still invisible but present Rena.

I will gladly take the bomb, Rena, Leroy answers. "Give it to me," he says loudly, ludicrous, as though the entity was hard of hearing. Is this also the test? Of course, it is, it all is, in its time.

Leroy feels the pressure in his gut, also the many-worlds excitement caused by the new arrival, enormous and so large as to be invisible to many of the worlds.

Inside his gut. I am the biggest! Leroy thinks, knowing the thought will be visible to something. Publication can't hold a candle to this! Leroy thinks.

Rena's face shows something like a smile. She is girlish, slim, browned like a nut. She has lost the absurd wig. She cradles a submachine gun as though it were her newborn infant. Perhaps it is.

At one and the same "time" Leroy rolls and capers with the current toward the sphincter, he is above it, observing the many separate universes, galaxies, larger assemblages. The dam is worlds-wide. Leroy is aware that he is like a ball of yarn, rolling up everything around, including the women, his dusty school, his lifetime of memories. The beggar sits caressing his dirty seamy face, as though he were a praying mantis cleaning up after a meal.

Everything moves, churns, rolls toward the dam of many worlds. The water is solid with creatures. Many more like him, Leroy observes, but they don't have his many-faceted ability to discern. Has the entity made him into a sibling-like creature? Did the ancients have a clue of this? They must have. I have to consult the books, Leroy thought, before he remembered his forward-momentumed progress, toward –

The Big Bang. The Big Bang!

Of course, starting over. The chief reason to do anything, proceeding from boredom with what is.

What the entity and I have in common, he

thought. Only that. But that's enough. But will I be allowed to live through it? Of course not. That's why I can actually start to see the worlds in the diverticuli, we are all being narrowed, rolled up into a ball, smaller than any ball ever rolled. Not to ask a question, no, the ball must be so small as to find a fissure, a crack, big enough to wiggle through. For the entity, having created the wall, must find a way to obey the laws it has built into it.

The crack, when it happened, was a disappointment. Just a crack. Not a world shattering, disequilibrating noise. Almost polite. On the other side, the bolus unwinds immediately, so immediately that it almost asks to be believed that it was always there, on the other side of the sphincter. A bit of humor on the part of the entity to objectify an event that has no parallel. Probably.

Even thinking about it, Leroy has to notice that he is still in one piece, so far as he can see. One piece, but of so many parts! Now he knows that with creation, has been created, re-created, multitudes of worlds. Worlds he cannot see, sense, imagine even. Except that he has been given an exemplary tour.

The other side of the Big Bang is our side. Leroy thrilled to the majesty of it all. At the same time hoping that the entity would not be bored anytime soon.

Meanwhile, the entity had forgotten about him in the excitement of creation. Leroy was bigger than galaxies laid end to end, actually as they were, in the beginning mini-moments on the other side of the Big Bang. Actually, in his shape, Leroy could be fairly certain he hadn't yet evolved on any of the slowly circling stars, acting as though they were members of an infinite ballet troupe.

No planets yet, of course, offspring of stars bumping into each other clumsily, unused to coming so close together.

Leroy would have to wait. How long? Hundreds of millions of years probably, even billions, until he could claim Belle again, now only an accumulation of dust. Maybe not even that. A sunbeam. But his own sunbeam.

The beggar spread his hands. To onlookers he was stretching. People were glad not to be anywhere close enough to smell his armpits. The entity has very, very smelly armpits, Leroy judged.

In order for an orderly universe to exist there must be an infinity of sweaty armpits.

Leroy decides a fiver might give him a chance of a fate better than the one he was experiencing.

# THE ARTISTS' SUITE

## DA VINCI SELFIE

When and where is your first memory? I ask this with a degree of animosity, as the following will seem totally insane to many of you who even impatiently sit down to read this.

Well, everything is insane if you focus on it. Just the fact that you are alive at this particular time and place rather than an infinity of others. The fact that you can read rather than sit drooling in an institution. Everything is unlikely.

So it was that Rhonda and I were among a throng wanting to get a closer look at La Gioconda and gave up at approximately the same time in disgust. We must have glanced at each other, though there is no memory of it. We decided, quite separately, to return to the museum precisely at its opening hour. Again, must have glanced at one another, making no note of it, only both our right hands holding our phones.

The next day we made our ways hurriedly up stairs, passing the incomplete statue of the Winged Victory with only a passing glance. That in itself is noteworthy. Ancient, powerful, reminiscent of so many battles – ho hum.

Never mind. Finally, at the hermetically enclosed and gasping-for-breath masterwork, alone together at last.

What do I mean, "together at last"? We were never together before. Holding up our cameras for the ultimate "selfie," we were together forever. And then, with a sudden kind of "dissolve," like when they flash back in movies, I was somewhere else, I had in my hand a stiff currying brush. I was finishing the rubdown of Da Vinci's best horse, one I alone was allowed to touch, of the painter's famously precise life. So many grooms had been dismissed, impatiently given the heave-ho by the painter. I would carefully tread the passageways to his door, to let him know the horse was ready for an afternoon peregrination. I hoped, as always, to be able to glance at the sleeping chambermaid, as carefully instructed what to dust as I was what to comb. Make it short. You are already bored. Leo was out and would be for hours. The cook never entered. The manservant also, he was with Leo. To make it short, again. We tussled on the floor, with only a dirty rag between us and hard rock, the covering of the room. So many hours of eye-glancing, notes passed between us, stuffed in corners. Servants like us were not permitted to touch, let alone...

We knew the portrait was inches away, face up, covered only with a light muslin, because Leo never felt it was finished.

And then he was dead and we were unemployed. But because the master didn't really value the unfinished oil, he rather casually willed it to me, in lieu of something really important.

The selfie. Did Rhonda know at that time we were reconstituted from those two, that we had thoroughly enjoyed each other, fully appreciative that each of us would ultimately wed another and would eventually meet again when we rushed upstairs this morning? That somehow, we were destined to destroy this bugaboo, this focus of so much attention that our singular and important qualities would go unrecognized?

How would we recognize our complicity? It comes through insanity. Only through one thing not following another is destiny fulfilled.

However, how could we actually meet, as we were in front of La Gioconda within our separate virtual realities? Our actual bodies in the matrix of the physical world were standing or sitting in our compartments, together with the thousands and thousands of other people in the world, locked up for life. It was after total enclosure by the masters, who gave us all our sustenance in return for absolute obedience. Our electrical sustenance that ran the machinery for the millions. Only for war, once or twice a generation, do we leave the total sustenance womb. We really look forward to war for that reason, as a relief from the tedium of affluence.

Was it a total accident that we would find each other virtually in front of the portrait that has meant so much to both of us? A terrific accident that can make a staggering difference. It is written somewhere that the machine will finally stop. We will slowly emerge and look around us at other thousands in each pod, and the pods in their thousands, millions, maybe even the overlords have no idea of how many, or exactly how it works, as it has worked smoothly for so many generations.

How will we get along, knowing nothing of how our meat and potatoes get generated. Animals? Virtual zoos have been the norm for so long we can't imagine actually touching one in the flesh.

Our selfies are just about to touch. They are within millimeters. I wildly wonder if there is a mechanism in place to stop this touch, which will be tantamount to the firing mechanism of the ancient atomic bomb, of which we have heard stories, fables, really, since most of it has to be exaggeration.

In the Louvre, in a former reconstitution, we discussed Bonaparte's bad breath and worse flatulence. We giggled over his standing to eat his sumptuous meals. Of course, we were glad he couldn't bear to stand in one place for long, which meant we got to eat very well.

We almost lost our lives once imitating him, me with my hand in my shirt, she with her smile behind a fan, imitating Josephine. He came in behind us, watched, and I am supposing, smiled, as he did not have us deported instantly.

We were sorry he lost his empire. We had hopes of being gentrified, even made into duke and duchess, allowed to marry, not merely cohabit.

Over all, the portrait loomed, and smiled her enigmatic smile. Rhonda and I knew what it meant. It meant only that the artist kept her posing on his little pedestal for too long and she had a desperate need to go to potty. She couldn't ask. She was embarrassed. She was too worried about her position, having married up, and up, and up, because of her beauty and the fact she brought no dowry to the marriage. She had to learn all the myriad ins and outs of the gentry.

That was the secret of the half-smile, the half-turn away from the artist. I can tell you she had more misery than just her bladder. She had a thing for Da Vinci. Did he know it? Absurd! Of course he did, but he couldn't let on. For one thing, he was more attracted to beings like myself. Why did he leave me the portrait if not?

She lives forever, even though Count Giocondo saw to it she was not able to continue flirting with even the stable boy. A much later poet saw into it and wrote the poem about a duchess.

Rhoda! Rode that sweet donkey around the property, smiling and waving at all of the personnel. Under my sweated brow I smiled back. She halted the donkey to inquire after my health, pretending a casual interest, under which the hot passion lay. How we were able to assuage that passion under sweet-smelling lilac bushes, knowing it was death for both of us if discovered.

I could see the swelling. The pride on the duke's face. My knowledge that my part in this beauty could never be acknowledged.

My work was as hard in the 'real' world. I had to sit down, take off the mask, register the regulation furniture, duplicated in countless square boxes. What if I opened a vein? Hopeless. A robot would charge into the room and staunch whatever wound I caused myself. And the demerits! No meat for a month!

Did you notice the switch from Rhonda to Rhoda? We are not precisely the same every time.

How did the painting get from Napoleon to the Louvre? How do you know it is actually there? To be truthful, it hasn't existed since 1911 when it was stolen and secreted out of the museum by a fanatically patriotic Italian, who was certain the thing belonged in an Italian museum. When he was finally hunted down, he decided to immolate himself along with the painting rather than give it up. In fact, charred remains were found clasped to his skeletal chest. Those of us in special cubicles can access the three-dimensional film of it. Can even participate by helping extinguish the flames and take home pieces of the picture.

Holograms. Rhea and I are supreme examples. Manifold copies, all of it available within a tiny area, living multiple variations of a life in many-storied stories.

Two of us witnesses to the infamous incident caused by those rabid painters, Apollinaire and Picasso, enflamed to be famous, bitter that the world's attention was centered on a five-hundred-year-old relic. I can reproduce the sarcastic dialogue between them, before they tore the thing apart, and then tore themselves apart. In a funnel of events leading to our time smiling in front of the selfie, another universe without the two artists. How many other duplets living lives of duplicity are there? Not my worry.

Between the two of us standing in front of the ridiculously guarded painted lady, nobody noticing how the young woman holding up the telephone, smiling into the uncaring lens, resembled the storied painting. Until I nudge her, pretending it to be an accident, rotating her gaze to take me in, my rigidly smiling face, inside of which I myself do not know the motive, yet acting out some ancient rite of passage. But passage to what end?

She was annoyed, but tried not to show it. The picture will be smudged, even a double exposure, though I believe such not possible with a phone camera. I can even see it in my mind's eye, the half-smiling, half-annoyed look, both regarding the picture, the artist and the interfering person, who is me. Another artist once accessed the situation, had a half-image of a stately pleasure dome, lost it to a waking knock to the door.

Leonardo did not have a high rank among the courtiers. Painters did not. Thus, the one portrayed, also not of singularly high importance even if she was the lady of the house, would not always be available. A serving maid would do: my Ruth, taken from her regular duties of slopping, sweeping, washing and hanging to dry. With her reddened hands on embarrassing view, Leo would have assured her that, like a magician, he could transform them into a lady's hands and fingers, unused to being immersed in anything less than warm and caressing.

As I jostled her, I could feel her softening appreciation of the artist, who had more than one motive in cozening her.

In fact, I felt my face reddening as he moved her here and there, touching her in pretense of positioning in a more favorable way.

Attraction was mutual. He was young enough to grow dizzy at her natural body heat and perfume that was able to penetrate the more stringent odors of the working girl.

And thus, several layers of woman, lady of the house and house servant, layer after layer, as the two became more and more entwined.

Five hundred years later, Ruth was re-entangled with me, the other servant, scorned at the time, now able to make myself felt. I wanted to chastise her for feeling she had risen far beyond her natural place. With me in my pod we can make a life better than she ever could have expected.

The crowd now surrounding us became silent as more and more of the people, with their own phones, turned their heads to look at her, whispering that she was the spitting image of the famous woman on the wall, whose gaze appeared to turn in the direction of Ruth. "Uncanny," murmured many. "Amazing, magical."

Of course, it was not amazing. She had merely modeled for the painting. I thought the picture would now surely disappear in a cloud of dust, having served its function of altering history.

What function? Napoleon's fall, the end of a monarchy, two painters in altercation that motivated many of their works, the rise of Mussolini in Italy, and countless other small adjustments that, like the butterfly's flutter, altered tides a thousand miles away.

I forcibly took her arm, pretty sure she would not resist or make a vocal fuss because she would have an inkling of the situation. "Think of the Chinese philosopher," I whispered, also almost certain she would cotton to the reference to the possibility that we were operating within a dream, or a dream within a dream, or even something entirely outside either of our understandings.

I had to be able to bring her to my own pod, along the way shedding years of history in the making, finding streets that would become covered over in buildings, in rubble, in silent ruin, before once more being built to accommodate the passive population of my time, bound to become hers.

She grew lighter as the miles extended. Lighter and stranger in size. Finally, when I was in front of the building, the elevator I had to take to my floor, I was able to look at her.

As I expected, she stared back out at me in mild astonishment, in a thickness that could be measured in millimeters, the only hope I could have for a living, breathing companion in the hologram. She had become once again the painting. The Mona Lisa of the museum was no more, any more than that the museum itself had become dust over centuries.

Hoping for a miracle, I clutched the antique and voiced in a hoarse voice my own floor.

# MUNCH AGONISTES

You see us, in the background. Non-threatening. Only a maniac would carry on so with us not even moving. Nothing is moving. Of course, that is the most threatening thing of all: not moving.

Even if you are a special person in your world, you naturally expect almost everything to move as usual. The worst thing would be to watch everything revolve around you in an ever-revolving circle as you are paralyzed and can only dumbly react.

That's not what is happening, either. I will try as to a very dense individual to try to make coherent, if not clear, what the world was like to such a person as Edvard Munch.

The first thing to note is that his entire life was leading up to the moments when he painted the self-portrait on the bridge. When he realized at last that the two who trailed him all of his life were closing in. We were ready to harvest the artist.

That really sounds good, doesn't it? Realize that the stalking can be really boring, tedious. If we moved in time it would have been intolerable. But we could hop and skip from one period to another. Changing our clothing, our skins, our attitudes now and then to please ourselves, keep ourselves fit.

He did insist on a small exchange. Something we could do with someone so paranoid and haunted. We could become flesh for him because he was so ready to hallucinate. Someone of his flesh is more able to rationalize what cannot ordinarily be visualized. So, we consented to model for him.

So many ways, so many ways. It was amusing. You have to see we don't really know our purpose. Purposes. Now and again someone pops up in the world, your world, whose composition calls for a more stringent cohesion. Usually, they fall apart early, because of the heat, too excessive for the species.

We were called to his side early. The parents issued the clarion. The specific fusion of genes in the womb, actually at the moment of contact, even before the penetration. We have to be called from a great distance – as you calibrate it, no distance at all as we note it. He would be stubborn, unable to cohere to the social metaphors. He would be looking wildly to the yonders for his life-mates. He would imagine that it was the sex he was lacking. Not, not that, a conjugal partner who would be able to tamp his fires when they burned too hot. When they would endanger his very existence, which he didn't really want anyway, as he saw the eternality of the visitors, us, and our equanimity, which he envied, though he also shuddered to think of.

That was his eternal agony, between wanting to live to create more, and the pain of it as much as he wanted it to end. And because of us he knew he was doomed or gifted to live to a fairly old age, into an age of existential horror such as he had envisioned all of his life.

This is what his sort considered the ability to look forward in time. No, it wasn't exactly that, not at all. It was a hallucination of the future. Like a nightmare, one he could control if he only were virtuous enough. Religious enough. Though he knew that was nonsense. But if he found a woman who was a believer, maybe he could hitch a ride on her solemnity.

But he had to laugh. It was the obverse of the scream, his ultimate statement, the one before we collected him in the fullness of his emotional, intellectual, and artistic growth. As we have collected many others. Actually, we are privileged to be the ones. Even if we don't like being painted. We did see to it we were only very fuzzy, in the background. All down the years – your years – we have managed to not really be seen, recognized for the same two.

In Cranach for example, or Picasso, you never know who we are. We politely request it. Actually, we require it. It's part of the agreement. Remember *Faust* by Goethe? A deal is a deal.

Among your sort, one of the elements making for the lushest work is confusion as to gender preference. With Munch he was forced to paint a female of perhaps fourteen years, not quite a woman, not yet finished with being a sexless male. His organs rose in terrified worship of that body. The genius of it is in its adoration of each of her lines, not yet having fallen into their final form. He could imagine embracing it as another unfinished body, not entering, not altering it, but embracing it almost as another serpent, limbless, all mouth and tongue.

Another portrait, with us in it, smiling, death and the maiden. He did this several times, several ways. He wanted death to come to the maiden. If he couldn't have her, then nobody could. And why not? Why couldn't he consummate his passion for the unformed girl? He was afraid of losing control, ability. Another artist embraced fanatical belief that orgasm meant losing a work of art. Quite funny. We had a very good time with that, then.

Death and the maiden. A very fertile line of creation. Remember, we are here to further, help mature and then harvest fruits. We are strictly adjured not to care about the emotional lives of artists. We are required to keep them to the straight and narrow.

Yes, he foresaw the advent of the Third Reich. He was terrified the Nazis would destroy his work. We tried to reassure him that it wouldn't happen. That, in the event, the Nazis would embrace him as one of their own. Like another northern artist, Sibelius. Quisling. Though that one was only an amateur painter. But this knowledge made him even more mad. In addition to his impotence, a very great addition to any artist's arsenal. Makes them literally crazy. They paint like mad to make up for it.

We gave Munch a large piece of equipment, allowed him some time to use it, with guilt, then in his later days took it away. Not literally. Just kept it pressed against his body, not erect. All those girls and women who streamed into his studio on the sea posed, naked, but inspired no heat in him. Remember the Hebrew king? We were there, too.

In the two figures, in the background, very discreet, two sinuous bodies, inside nearly naked, even at that distance, our combined odor, call it scent, pouring out for him a visible column of pure physical attraction, in all its symphonic harmony and dissonance, almost impossibly calling him to turn around, look at us, roll pell-mell to us, to try to meld himself into us, die, perhaps, see us as the very last things in his protuberant eyeballs.

What we had not yet decided, even in that moment, was whether to allow him to touch us, our luscious erect nipples, suck on them as he was never allowed by his soon-dead mother. Move down our bodies, one after the other, to nuzzle our belly buttons, visualizing the invisible connections to the absent mother. Always absent mother, the suckling one, never having had enough of.

And then down, lower, to the thicket of purest scent, intoxicated even while horrified and standing away from us. At the same time holding us by our buttocks, pressing thickets together, forests of wildly abundant life, so intoxicating as to cause almost instant death.

But no. We are not finished with him. Agony of frustration creates its own life. Withholding, separation, the electricity arcs over separation. We need Munch electric.

The mouth opens in a rictus of horror, agony, despair, longing. Every viewer in the world autonomously feels it in his or her gut, produces his or her art.

That's why there are thousands of imitations,

cartoon, spoofs of this self-portrait of the artist. Everybody is forced to identify with it. It is our greatest success in millennia.

He was forced to live with it. We are not pointlessly cruel, but only to a purpose. The stream of models eager to pose, to open their bodies to the great man, caused only bitterness with him. "Why weren't they available when I was young, when I could have done something with them?"

Done what, Mr. Genius? We ask you. Wasn't it better than nothing to continue after that terrible afternoon, terrible for you, that is, not for the world, which has appreciated it forever after, maybe even the Nazi naysayers.

The work even contributed to their ultimate failure, Edvard. Yes, and how was that? Deep in the twisted psyche of the most inveterate Nazi was fear of impotence. After the posturing, swaggering, the use of weapons in place of genitals, we expanded the fear, the fanaticism, unfocusing their aim so that even their biggest weapons went astray as to their missiles.

It wasn't the terror, finally, with Munch. He ultimately accepted his essentially neutered portraits. You don't get to see them unless you ask specifically at the museum named after him. His father would have blinked. His mother held her breasts as though they would fly away from her.

Perhaps to him? The incest greed? We haven't spoken of that, but it was always there, in the females struggling to get away from the main figure. We are on both sides. We take no side. We have no position. We are merely there to pull Edvard's soul from its position in the solar plexus. Cause it to spin frantically, thereby creating torque, and finally the energy for which we have been placed here.

Ultimately, the horse. The uncut version of Edvard himself. We gave him that. With the nubile girls, the adept horse kept him company in the last years. He was able to help it mate with a succession of mares. The artist himself allowed the image of lust to bloom in him, for the mares.

And they were beautiful. Those mares! All palominos. Blonde fetlocks, which swung like incredibly endowed teenage girls, too young to be dangerous. Not like that woman in the hotel. He was trapped there with her, while she wildly, furiously blamed him for his useless appendage.

He pleaded with her for time, for patience. He would tell her what to do. She was adamant. It would have to be man to woman to man, just the two of them, no outside aids. No stallion mating with a gorgeous palomino outside the window.

Endless partial portraits of her. Some with death, which he wished her, heartily. But then blamed himself. Cursed himself. Consigned himself to a paradise of flame.

With his oversized organ going up like an exuberant torch, for once and for all spurting a flammable liquid that douses everything around, including his horde, his store, of paintings.

If he cannot erect himself, let everything fall into flame.

Well, of course, we could not allow that. He had a peaceful verdant ending, with images of a shouting loving audience, in front of a vast mural of life itself, painted by him with great care and love. His last work. His enduring work.

We gave it to him. After all the agony he deserved it.

THE END

# L'ORIGINE DU MONDE

Even among us it is uncertain whether Dali was chosen one of the thirty-six or if he chose himself, slipped under the rope, so to speak, before anyone could stop him.

It would get worse before it got better. That is, came under control. In every generation a powerhouse arises, a whirlwind of energy and ego almost unstoppable. Then, the powers that be observe a direction the person has taken and actually urge him or her onward to the chosen place. This way everybody is satisfied that he or she has won, regardless of the decision.

An example, in case the above is a bit fuzzy. The Black Death, bubonic plague. It started with one bacterium flexing its muscles, applying for greater amplitude. Its mutterings and blusterings became too much and so one of us allowed it scope, reproduction, finally decimation to the world. The rest had to justify the obvious slaughter, so it became the basis for greater peasant freedom, higher wages, the growth of representative government.

Also the thirty-six. From time to time there was muttering even among them. Too little to do. With the threat of one of them becoming supreme over all the rest, as mutating they are and have to be. The one become the messiah remains constant over ages. So, you can see that would be a plum position and all of them quietly jockeying for it. Quietly, because it would be unseemly to be jostling one another.

Rather unusual for the species was his realization of the teeming life inside his body, which he visualized in the form of ants. Ants emerging from the palm of a hand in an early film he made with another artist. The film aroused so much energy that it came to our attention. But it was already too late. He had elbowed his way into the group of thirty-six. Particularly outrageous, as nobody had died and he became the thirty-seventh, absolutely out of the question. But there he was, sitting smug and snug.

Then it was going to be the problem of how to get rid of him. He was canny. He partook of our knowledge to keep himself alive, prosperous, visible. We couldn't simply throw a rope around his neck and take him off the world stage when he was always so confoundedly present!

It became a game of hide and seek. He was able to marshal the ants, not really ants but energy packets that emerged from many of his works, most visibly the most famous oil with the melting pocket watch. Nobody is able to see any of us emerging with the mass of them, which is entirely how we wanted it.

Trying to regain some measure of control, after all. Petulant, we cannot be. It got worse.

Secretly, after pretending to be a socialist, a syndicalist, a communist, he made common cause with the emerging strong man, Franco, who was bidding to overthrow the elected government of Spain and install himself as absolute ruler, to mirror the total dictator of Germany almost next door, Hitler in Germany. What Franco didn't know is that Dali planned to usurp Franco and run the country himself. To this presumption, he undertook to paint a series of flattering portraits of Franco, urging him to take them, gratis, something he never, never did.

Franco was of course flattered. He placed them everywhere in his palace, something Dali envied. What Franco didn't know was that, like Da Vinci's Mona Lisa, there was an under-painting. Invisible. But the portrait underneath was of a doddering old man, close to death, diseased, hopeless. Dali hoped and planned for a kind of sympathetic magic. In this case greatly unsympathetic. An idea he got from Oscar Wilde in his novel, *The Picture of*

*Dorian Gray*. Not that Dali ever read anything. No, indeed, that would imply someone else knew something he didn't. His ego was such.

No, the one who read the book was Gala. His Gala. The Gala he stole from a fellow artist, helpless against Dali's greater magnetism. Able, as it turned out, to win her back from time to time when Dali deliberately turned off the current. We were able to manage that. That being to make female organs so obnoxious to him that his terrific volume was negated. That was, mercifully, what kept him from grasping messiah-hood from the other thirty-six.

Am I getting beyond myself? When past, present and future are thoroughly muddled it is almost impossible to keep things in order for you.

How did the forlorn poet do it? Quite simple, as it turned out. Gustave Courbet merely lent him his painting, *L'Origine du Monde*, a very realistic portrait of the florid pubis of a young woman, in full bloom. Dali saw myriad ants emerging from her crotch, all of them crawling toward him, bent on his destruction. He got down on his knees to Paul Éluard, the name of the poet, pleading with him to take Gala for as long as he wished, to do with her as he wanted.

This was OK with Gala, who was possessed of an insatiable sexual itch. She could barely contain herself not to fall on her former husband right there, right in front of the terrified Dali.

This caused some satisfaction among us, you may be sure, but it was nothing permanent. Not enough.

The paintings that followed continued his upward climb. Franco, however, did not shrivel. Sympathetic magic was drivel. Dali decided to become so rich nobody would be able to withstand him. He turned to advertising, marketing, modeling. But Gala was so crazy she had to be confined in a castle as close to Franco's as possible. Much expense.

Bad times. His association with Franco cost him all his former friends. He was alone with the mad woman, who allowed him admittance to the castle only on designated days, when her bully-boys were not servicing her insatiable body. And then, when he was allowed entrance, he was greeted with numerous copies of the Courbet insult, and Gala's own sadly depleted pubis, withered legs and dangling breasts.

Dali was both magnetized and repelled. She fed him quantities of hokum medicines, sickening his always-stalwart body, wearing it down.

But not soon enough. Hitler had killed off almost all of the thirty-six. In fact, only Dali was left. He was so close to becoming the messiah!

There could be nothing we could do about it. And the job has no time limit. It's forever!

Gala died. Dali lingered. The procession was getting closer to him, full of glitter and glory, pulsing with the energy of infinite space and time.

He could feel it. His pace multiplied. Elephants, horses, the Virgin in space. He could visualize worlds and creatures nobody else could. He was increasingly amazing. We held nothing back from him, now that we were relatively sure he would fade before the immortals reached him.

Probably there was never any real possibility. Just a greater power having its fun with us, being bored with everything always being predictable, immutable.

THE END

EYEWEAR PUBLISHING